BERANI

PRAISE FOR

Music for Tigers

⊁ Green Earth Book Award honor book ⊰
⊁ OLA Forest of Reading Silver Birch Award honour book ⊰
⊁ Finalist for the MYRCA Sundogs Award ⊰
⊁ Finalist for the Rocky Mountain Book Award ⊰
⊁ *Kirkus Reviews* Best Middle Grade Book of the Year ⊰
⊁ USBBY Outstanding International Book ⊰
⊁ Junior Library Guild selection ⊰
⊁ *Washington Post KidsPost* Summer Book Club selection ⊰
⊁ White Ravens Selection ⊰

"Conservation, neurodiversity, and history intersect
in surprising and authentic ways."—*Kirkus* ★ **Starred Review**

"A story straight out of adolescent daydreams."
—*Shelf Awareness* ★ **Starred Review**

"A coming-of-age story with a conservation twist."
—*Foreword Reviews* ★ **Starred Review**

"Kadarusman continues to be a clear, insightful,
and humourous guide."—*Quill & Quire* ★ **Starred Review**

"A love letter to the unique flora and fauna of the
Tasmanian Tarkine."—*Booklist*

"A balanced and comprehensible voice to the environmental
discussion for young people."—*School Library Journal*

PRAISE FOR

Girl of the Southern Sea

⟶ Finalist for the Governor General's Literary Award ⟵
⟶ Honorable Mention for the NCTA Freeman Book Award ⟵
⟶ Honor Book for the Malka Penn Award for Human Rights
in Children's Literature ⟵
⟶ Finalist for the SYRCA Diamond Willow Award ⟵
⟶ USBBY Outstanding International Book ⟵
⟶ Rise: A Feminist Book Project List selection ⟵
⟶ Bank Street Best Book ⟵
⟶ Junior Library Guild selection ⟵

"With nuanced characters, this is a lovely gem for fans
of irrepressible girls."—**Booklist**

"A gripping, emotional realistic novel describing the grim
realities of growing up in Indonesian poverty."
—**School Library Journal**

"Readers will cheer Nia's real powers—her storytelling talent
and her resiliency—in this vividly set story."
—**The Horn Book Guide**

"A thought-provoking peek into a culture deserving of more
attention in North America."—**Kirkus Reviews**

"An uplifting novel about hope and the power
of storytelling."—**Foreword Reviews**

BERANI

By Governor General's Award Finalist
Michelle Kadarusman

pajamapress

www.pajamapress.ca   info@pajamapress.ca

 Canada Council Conseil des arts
for the Arts   du Canada

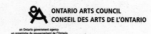 ONTARIO ARTS COUNCIL
CONSEIL DES ARTS DE L'ONTARIO
an Ontario government agency
un organisme du gouvernement de l'Ontario

 Canada

The publisher gratefully acknowledges the support of the Canada Council for the Arts and the Ontario Arts Council for its publishing program. We acknowledge the financial support of the Government of Canada through the Canada Book Fund (CBF) for our publishing activities.

Library and Archives Canada Cataloguing in Publication
Title: Berani / by Governor General's award finalist Michelle Kadarusman.
Names: Kadarusman, Michelle, 1969- author.
Description: First edition.
Identifiers: Canadiana 20220150028 | ISBN 9781772782608 (hardcover)
Classification: LCC PS8621.A33 B47 2022 | DDC jC813/.6—dc23Publisher

Cataloging-in-Publication Data (U.S.)
Names: Kadarusman, Michelle, 1969-, author.
Title: Berani / Michelle Kadarusman.
Description: Toronto, Ontario Canada : Pajama Press, 2022. | Summary: "Perspectives of two Indonesian middle-schoolers and a caged orangutan entwine. Wealthy Malia faces the consequences of disobediently circulating an anti-palm-oil petition at her school, resulting in suspensions for herself, her best friend, and her teacher. Ari, fortunate to be plucked from his impoverished village to attend school and compete in chess tournaments, helps the uncle who is hosting him but worries about Ginger Juice, the orangutan his uncle keeps in a cage. When Ari learns about orangutan rehabilitation centers from Malia's petition, the young people unite to plot a rescue"— Provided by publisher.
Identifiers: ISBN 978-1-77278-260-8 (hardcover)
Subjects: LCSH: Middle school students – Indonesia – Juvenile fiction. | Environmental responsibility – Juvenile fiction. | Orangutans – Juvenile fiction. | Animal rescue – Juvenile fiction. | BISAC: JUVENILE FICTION / Science & Nature / Environment. | JUVENILE FICTION / Animals / Apes, Monkeys, etc. | JUVENILE FICTION / Social Themes / Values & Virtues.
Classification: LCC PZ7. K333Ber | DDC [F] – dc23

Cover art by Peggy Collins
Cover and book design— Lorena González Guillén

Manufactured by Friesens
Printed in Canada

Pajama Press Inc.
11 Davies Avenue, Suite 103, Toronto, Ontario Canada, M4M 2A9

Distributed in Canada by UTP Distribution
5201 Dufferin Street Toronto, Ontario Canada, M3H 5T8

Distributed in the U.S. by Ingram Publisher Services
1 Ingram Blvd. La Vergne, TN 37086, USA

 MIX
Paper from
responsible sources
FSC® C016245

For my brother Andre

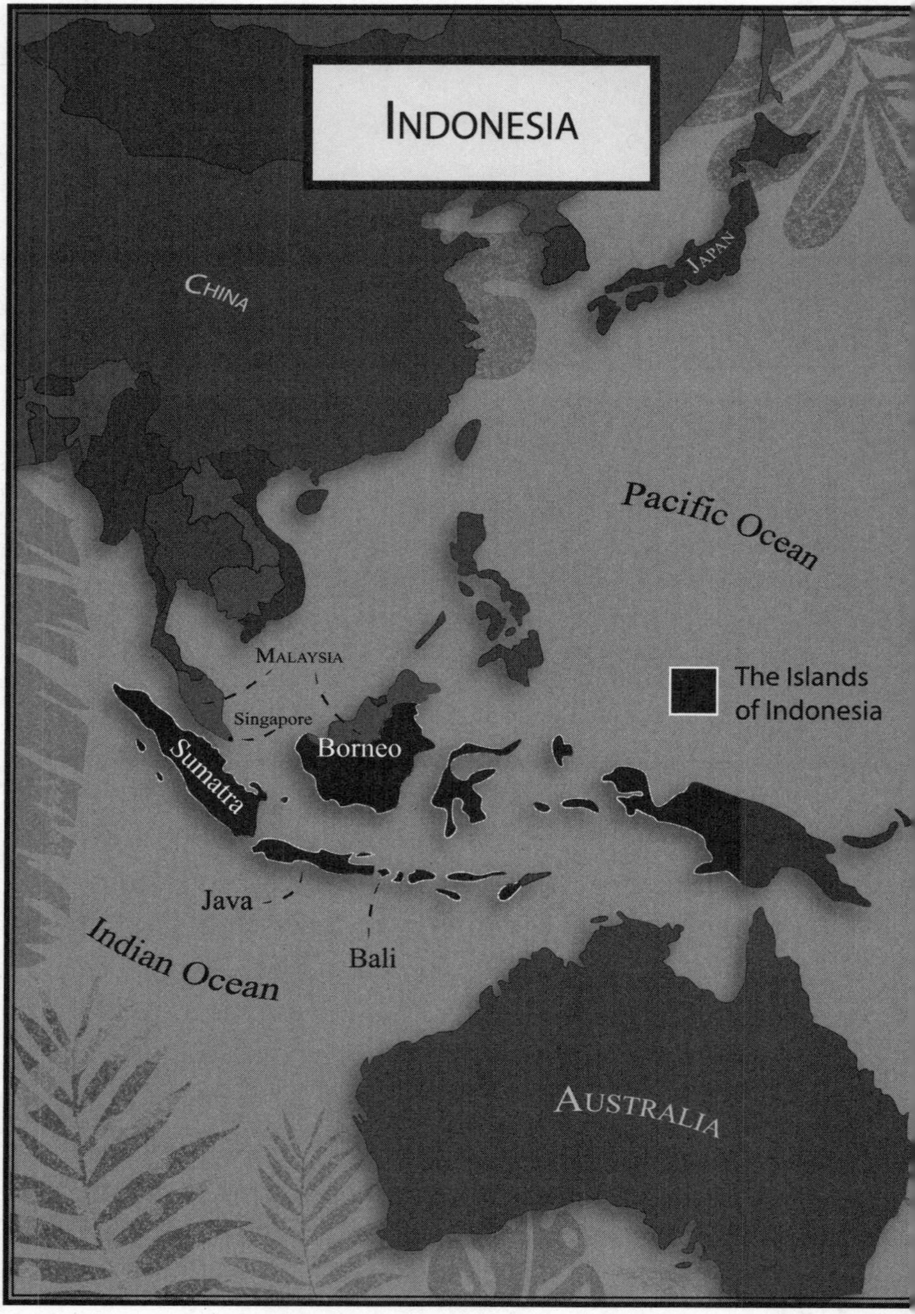

INDONESIA

CHINA

JAPAN

Pacific Ocean

MALAYSIA

Singapore

Borneo

The Islands
of Indonesia

Sumatra

Java

Bali

Indian Ocean

AUSTRALIA

Malia

I take a deep breath and begin to speak.

"Listen. Impossible things happen all the time. Strange, mysterious, and fantastic stuff unfolds right under our noses every day.

Take, for example, miniature elephants.

Fact: fossil remains of prehistoric dwarf elephants, called Stegodons, have been found on many islands here in Indonesia. These creatures were the size of a Saint Bernard dog and even had tusks.

I am not kidding you! The scientists say this species lived at the same time as early humans. Can you believe that?! Imagine having a mini-elephant as your family pet?

It only seems impossible because you never saw them.

But what if I told you, that right this very minute, a creature that shares nearly 97% of our human DNA (but is seven times stronger) is living in the treetops, eating fruit and leaves, playing, crying, laughing, raising babies, and sleeping in giant nests hundreds of feet about the ground? That a tribe of copper-haired forest people lives peacefully above us in the towering canopies of Sumatra and Borneo.

And then, what if I told you that we humans are destroying this creature's home and, along with it, some of the richest and most diverse rainforests on the planet? Just because we humans think that an oil used to make lipsticks, chocolates, and a million other throwaway items is more important.

Impossible? No. It is happening as I tell you this. The product is called palm oil and it is causing deforestation and the extinction of orangutans. It is happening right here in our own country."

I put down my presentation notes and meet Mom's gaze. "Then I'll show the Greenpeace video and hand out my petition to protest the banning of palm-free product labels in our supermarkets," I tell her. "How does it sound? What do you think?" I ask. "I still have more to write. I know it's too short."

"It's fantastic. I mean it, Malia. It's really amazing." Mom's brow creases. "But have you told your teacher what you will be presenting? Does she know you will be asking the students to sign a petition?"

"She said we could do a ten-minute presentation on a subject of our choice and that we could also include digital visuals."

"It's a complicated problem, sweetheart. In Indonesia, especially, it is an explosive subject. Likely some of the children at your own school have families who rely on palm oil agriculture. There is a lot more to the issue. It's not black and white."

"It is to me," I say.

"I just worry that the subject might cause some of the kids to be, well, conflicted." Mom gives me a half smile. "They are only thirteen-year-olds after all. They're not the ones making the decisions."

"But that's exactly the point!" I say throwing up my hands. "We should be properly informed on product labels so we can at least make informed decisions about what we buy. That is how we seventh graders *can* make a difference."

Mom moves forward to cup my face in her hands.

"Yes, you can make a difference. Of course, you can. And I am very, very proud of you. But please do me this one favor."

She locks eyes with me. "Tell your teacher what you are planning to do before you go ahead with your presentation, OK? I don't want you to get yourself into trouble over it."

"True activists don't care about getting into trouble," I say.

Mom shoots me a warning look.

"OK, OK, I promise."

"Thank you," she says, kissing my forehead, not noticing my fingers are crossed behind my back.

Mom has been easier on me than usual, ever since she told me about wanting to move us back to her home in Toronto, Canada. She thinks that I can be jollied into a good mood, like when I was a little girl. Well, I'm not a little girl anymore, and I am not—not ever, ever, ever—going to leave Surabaya. This is my home. This is where my best friend is, where my school is, and where I want to live forever. Here is where Papa is buried, and where I go and sit by his grave under the mango trees and talk to him; tell him all about the petitions and letters I have started for the orangutans.

Just yesterday I read a magazine article to Papa about the Swedish climate-change activist Greta Thunberg and her Fridays For Future movement. Greta is a person who does what she sets out to do. She forced people to listen, even when she was younger than I am now.

How can I save the orangutans if I'm all the way over in Canada?

Leave Indonesia? It is just not going to happen. I don't want to listen to what Mom says about how, with Papa gone, she wants to be with her own family back in Toronto.

BERANI

"It's been two years now since Papa died, Malia," she said. "It's time for us to go home to Canada."

"Home?" I said. "But I am already home. Indonesia *is* home."

Ari

The famous *Warung Malang* is my uncle's restaurant. He started it when he was a skinny young man with a full head of hair. Uncle Kus is quite bald now, and quite chubby too, but he is happily so. He says people trust a bald cook with a big belly. That's just the way it is.

Uncle opened the restaurant as a roadside food stall, selling *sop buntut*, oxtail soup. That is his main specialty. Uncle worked hard, day and night, selling sop buntut from his food stall and he made a name for himself as having the best oxtail soup in all of Malang. His secret is the rich broth that he simmers all day on the stove top. It bubbles away, filled with ox bones, garlic, and cinnamon. People come from all over Malang for it. Some patrons tell us they cannot find a better soup, even in Surabaya, a larger city an hour away. Over the years, Uncle was able to upgrade from a simple food stall to a real restaurant with a ceramic tiled floor, rattan chairs, and twelve tables where his customers are able to sit, relax, and slurp his prized soup for breakfast and lunch.

At Warung Malang we not only have comfortable furnishings. We also have live attractions. A mynah bird called Elvis Presley and an orangutan named Ginger Juice. Ginger Juice is named after Uncle's other house specialty. It's a drink made from freshly squeezed *jeruk* and grated ginger. Jeruk is a locally grown citrus. The fruit is something of a cross between an orange and a mandarin with a bright green peel. It's wonderfully refreshing and blends beautifully with the spiciness of fresh ginger root. The drink is served in a tall glass over crushed ice with a spoonful of cane sugar to bring out the tangy sweetness. With her bright orange hair, Ginger Juice is well named, especially as she lives full-time at the restaurant. She and Elvis Presley, are our small team of mascots at Warung Malang.

The animal cages sit on the grassy area in view of the covered eating pavilion so the patrons can be entertained by Elvis Presley's singing "You Ain't Nothin' But A Hound Dog." The children never tire of slipping small bananas into Ginger Juice's cage to watch her delicately peel and eat them. Lately though, she sits for long periods with her back to the patrons, lazily scratching and grooming her fur.

BERANI

My family has sent me to stay with Uncle, so I can attend the local middle school. I am grateful, of course. I am lucky to have a successful uncle living close to the city center where I can attend a good school. Our village school only goes until the end of the elementary grades. Naturally, I must make myself useful to Uncle. There are many chores to balance his generosity.

Every morning before school, I must check that Elvis Presley has water and clean newspaper in his cage. Every day after school, I must do the accounting and bookkeeping for Uncle. But of all my chores and schoolwork, there is one task I dread more than any other, and that is looking after Ginger Juice.

Uncle says that she is lucky he got her when she was a baby, after her mother was killed in the jungle. She would surely have died alone in the forest. Here at the restaurant, she is given as much papaya and banana as she wishes and she is safe from poachers and forest fires. She is allowed to grow fat and lazy. She is adored by the restaurant patrons. But she is also in a cage.

When she first came as a baby, she didn't live in the cage. She was held and cuddled and slept in the house, just like a real baby. I didn't live here then, but when we came to visit, my cousin and I would play with her. Ginger Juice tumbled and rolled around on the grass and climbed whatever she could reach. She would pull funny faces with her wide, flat lips and slap her furry belly, making us laugh. But as she grew older and stronger, she became harder to control. She would throw things and often climb onto the roof. Sometimes it would take hours for her to come down again. Uncle started keeping her in the cage for longer and longer periods. "It's for her own good," he would say. "One day she might climb over the fence and not come back. She could wander off and get run over by a truck."

That was years ago. Now she never leaves the cage. In fact, she can no longer fit through the door for she has far outgrown the opening.

Maybe Uncle does not notice her eyes the way I do. She watches me. Silently watches. I keep my head down as I hose out her cage and lay clean newspaper, causing my reading glasses to slide down my nose. "We must always keep her cage spick and span," says Uncle.

I push my glasses back in place and try not to look into Ginger Juice's eyes as I work.

But sometimes I can't help it. Her gaze catches me. And it jogs something in me that I don't want to think of, a feeling I can't shake.

Ginger Juice

Drip. Drip. Drip.

Fat raindrops *tap, tap, tap* on fingers. Elvis Presley, black bird, sings secret song. Song he crows when no human here. When human here, he moves up, down on perch and sings human words over and over.

When Elvis sings secret music, I remember birdsong from before-life. Scraps of sound and scent dance out of reach, same like butterflies used to flutter over nest. When Elvis Presley sings secret song, I back in green, swaying world with smell of wet leaves and moss.

And you, *Ibu*. You there too.

When it rains you show me how keep dry with giant taro leaf hold over head. All mothers show babies these things.

The small male human comes to sweep cage. Elvis Presley stops secret song. I watch human move around. The small human cleans cage now. Not big, round human anymore. Small human is skinny like mongoose. Big human calls him boy. Boy has something on his face. Rings over eyes like a slow loris.

When he comes close, I smell his fear. He not look at me. He push slow-loris rings up nose and keep head down.

I watch him for many raindrops, then haze comes to take me. It easy when haze comes. Haze slips over head like hood humans put on Elvis Presley cage. Haze change heartbeat of time. It let me forget. The haze let my head slip away. Far, far away. And fear feelings get dim. Dim. Dimmer.

I rub fingers together. Wet. Lift to lips.

Lick. Lick. Sniff. Sniff.

Bad. Bitter. Stink.

Rain tastes like air here, but little bit sweet too. Rain is free. Rain falls where it wants. Rain-scent holds me back from haze today and do not want me forget before-life.

You and me, Ibu. We together and we free.

Malia

Bibi shuffles into my dark bedroom and whistles at me to wake up as she pulls the curtains open.

"Look at you, still in bed," she says. "Do you think you are royalty? Half the day has gone already. Get up."

I look at the clock. It is 6 a.m. The school day begins early in Surabaya, so students can be done before the searing heat of early afternoon.

Our housemaid, Bibi, is notoriously bad tempered. She often says I put on royal airs. Her default mood is surly. My friends are scared of her. Actually, come to think of it, pretty much everyone is scared of her. Even Mom. The only person who wasn't scared of her was Papa. And me, of course. Bibi was Papa's *amah* when he was a boy and she's been my nanny since I was born. She is quite ancient.

I stretch my arms to the ceiling and swing my feet to the floor where Bibi has deftly kicked my slippers. "Don't dirty my floor," she mutters, but we both know she really means keep your feet warm and cozy. Bibi shuffles back out the door, *tsk-tsking* in my direction. "Wash up," she says. "Your *bubur* is getting cold."

I remember with a sudden thump in my chest that today is the day of my presentation. I go to my bathroom and splash water on my face. I peer at myself in the mirror. "Time to save the world!" I tell my reflection. The girl in the mirror stares back at me challengingly. She lifts her chin with an air of confidence, but the girl inside quivers a little.

I dress in my school uniform, a white blouse and pale blue skirt, and go to sit at the breakfast table. Bibi lifts the plate she has put over my bowl of bubur to keep it from going cold. The warm chicken porridge is creamy with the perfect amount of salt and crunchy, fried shallots on top, just how I like it. I look toward Mom's bedroom, but the door is closed. Since Papa died, Mom usually has her breakfast in her room. Bibi takes her a tray with sweet, black tea and sliced mango with yogurt.

Morning is when Mom calls one of her brothers or my grandparents in Canada. It is twelve hours behind there, so our morning is their evening. Sometimes I'll take my bowl of bubur and sit on the big bed with Mom and listen while she chats with her family. Her English sounds different when she speaks with her brothers. The words are so fast that they blur together like a song. And sometimes she uses words that I don't know. "It's just slang," she'll tell me afterwards. "It's not proper English." She should know. She is a linguistics professor. She speaks perfect Bahasa, but we speak English together. I know that my English is fluent, better than my classmates', but I still feel embarrassed when I speak to my Canadian cousins. When I was little, they would always make fun of my accent. "It's so cute," they'd say, "how you roll your *Rs*." Another reason I don't want to move to Toronto. I imagine an entire classroom laughing at my accent. A whole school full of girls, like my cousins with their silky blonde hair and pale skin, pointing and telling me I'm *cute*, in that mocking way you speak to a baby. "Who cares about an accent?" Mom says. "Anyway, it's true, you *do* sound cute."

Grrr.

I take another mouthful of bubur. Today is not a day to be cute. Today I'm going to be taken dead seriously.

Ari

I admit I find it difficult to put my whole heart into the restaurant chores when there are other things I could be doing, like playing chess. This morning I must leave early as, against all odds, I have been chosen to represent the school on our chess team in a tournament at a private school in Surabaya. I've only started playing since beginning middle school, but my friend Faisel says I have natural talent. We play together at least three times a week. We have an arrangement that I pay for Faisel's coffee and pastry at the *Warung Kopi,* and he gives me chess pointers. Faisel has been playing since he was a young child, and his guidance has helped a lot.

Michelle Kadarusman

We don't have a chess master at school, just a bossy senior named Yosef who runs the club. He stalks around the players and groans loudly if he sees one of us make a bad move. Or he will slap his forehead. It isn't a perfect learning environment for chess, but the game continues to intrigue me. The endless possibilities! The endless strategies! Yosef has stood behind my chair a number of times now, without groaning or slapping his forehead. At the last club meeting he raised his eyebrows and nodded, saying, "Stable move." I hope my enthusiasm for the game has earned his favor.

By far the best players are two girls, Melonie and Samir. No one can touch them. They hover above us mortals like celestial beings. And it should be them, of course, representing our school instead of me, but a small miracle occurred last week. The miracle coming in the shape of a highly contagious, but not life-threatening, bout of strep throat that wrought havoc among our chess members. Half of the players, including Melonie and Samir, are down with it.

I look around the restaurant to check that I've done enough sweeping to keep me from Uncle's bad books. Despite the rain, the heat is rising. Moisture clings to my clothes from the effort of my sweeping. I decide I've done enough to stay out of trouble, so I store the broom and collect my school satchel. Elvis Presley watches me, his small head cocked. He begins to bob up and down on his perch as I approach, seeming to rev up for one of his musical numbers. "Have a good day, Elvis," I say as I pass. Ginger Juice is watching the rain, her eyes blinking slowly. She has slipped her huge hand through the bars to touch the raindrops. When I look at her, that lurking feeling stabs at me again. I recognize it, that feeling. It's the feeling of betraying a friend. Something I know well.

I step out into the soft *pitter-patter* of raindrops and hold my satchel above my head to keep my white school shirt from getting soaked. I try to dispel the memories. *Pull yourself together, Ari. Ginger Juice is just an ape. She isn't a friend at all, or even human. She isn't Suni.*

It would be accurate to say that Suni was, until recently, my best friend. My childhood pal, my cousin, my co-conspirator of village high jinks, my rice paddy partner in crime. But I am here in Malang studying, while she is back in the village. No doubt, right now, she is ushering the ducks along the lines of narrow dirt mounds among the rice paddies, calmly encouraging them to fill their bellies with the slugs that will otherwise eat the tender shoots. Or perhaps she is knee-deep in mud, twisting strands of rice saplings into the earth with her delicate fingers. In elementary school she was the clever one, not me, but I'm attending middle school, not her. I took the only place our family can afford. I stole the one chance she will ever have of continuing school. Instead, she is the one who is left behind to help tend the rice fields.

I have not visited home, as I had promised her I would do, since moving to Malang. "Come home often and tell me every-thing you are learning," she had urged. "Bring me your books, show me your lessons. I might be able to keep up! Promise you won't forget me."

At first, I was too busy balancing schoolwork and the restaurant chores. But then, when the opportunity and time presented itself, something else stopped me.

Guilt. Guilt stopped me.

How could I go back to the village and explain the wide horizon of experiences the city has opened for me? New friends, study, and chess. It is everything we had dreamed it would be. Only, it is my dream alone now, and no longer the dream that we shared as children. The more time that passes, the more distant my former life in the rice fields becomes. And the easier it is to tell my family, yet again, that I am too busy. That I cannot return. The more time that passes, the more distance I can put between Suni and me and pretend it doesn't matter, and that she is happy where she is. The more time passes, I can pretend that I haven't betrayed her.

This balancing act of the mind is all manageable, except when I look at Ginger Juice. Seeing the ape slumped in her cage, my carefully buried feelings come tumbling out, demanding attention. I shake my head. Better to focus on other things. Keep busy. If I fill my mind enough, I can bury the guilt deep enough for it never to surface.

Malia

Bibi hands me my school satchel.

"No lunch, right?" I ask her.

She gives me a dismissive wave. Since starting middle school, I have explained to her that I prefer to eat at the school cafeteria rather than bring my own lunch every day. The cafeteria is the place to be at lunchtime, although not so much for the food it is fair to say. Bibi has not taken the news well. She watches me intently as I step through our front security gate. The hot, muggy air envelopes me. Surabaya is relentlessly steamy no matter the time of day. I call to one of the *becak* drivers on the corner. School is too far to walk

31

and too close to be driven. The perfect distance for a pedicab, especially when it's wet. The morning's rain persists, making the air smell like over-ripe papaya. I climb up onto the worn vinyl seat that the driver has dried off with an old towel. The becak's canopy protects me from the drizzle. The old pedicab's wheels squeak as the driver pedals toward school. I wait until we are a safe distance from home before peeking into my satchel. Just as I suspected, Bibi has smuggled inside a familiar plastic container. I sigh and reach in to open it. *Mie goreng.* She knows very well fried noodles are my favorite. And she has even added the tiny shrimp I love. I push the plastic container aside to make sure I have my presentation notes along with the USB key that holds the Greenpeace video I plan to show after my speech. I have printed paper copies of my petition but I've also created an online form that I can direct students to.

"Impossible things happen all the time. Strange, mysterious and fantastic stuff unfolds right under our noses every day." I speak the sentences aloud, practicing the first lines of my presentation again to help soothe my nerves. I conjure images of the stolen forests and the innocent orangutans having their homes and their lives snatched away from them. By the time the becak reaches school, my nerves have given way to simmering anger and indignation for the apes.

My best friend, Putu, is waiting for me at our usual spot by the cherry-red bougainvillea bush outside the schoolyard. She is holding an umbrella and hopping excitedly from one foot to the other. "It's your presentation today!" she announces.

BERANI

Since childhood, Putu has taken on the role of commentator to my every move. She finds the goings-on of my life more interesting than her own. Or maybe it's because she has enough kindness to fill a football stadium. Once I told her she was too kind for her own good, and she said "It's just as well because you aren't always nice, so between the two of us, we balance things out." I cannot argue with her logic. I know Putu is my one true friend, and this knowledge is enormous.

"Yes," I say, handing the becak driver his fare. "I'm ready."

Putu is a head shorter than I am and she wears her hair in a bob that bounces prettily as she trots next to me, struggling to keep pace. We enter the gates to our school, *Sekolah Menegah Pertama* (SMP). It's a private school, but unlike the private international schools, our lessons are taught in Bahasa, not English. Most people think that all Indonesians are Muslim, but there is a small population of other faiths in our school. Our student population is made up of mixed religions, Muslim of course, but also Christian, Buddhist, and Hindu. In Indonesia you have to declare a religion, even if you don't go to church or mosque or temple. Mom says it is different in Canada. There you don't have to state your beliefs. Putu is Hindu, because her parents are from the island of Bali, where most people are Hindu. I don't have a religion, but on school papers I tick the Christian box, which I figure at least entitles me to the Christmas gifts my Canadian grandparents send me each year.

I thrust a few petitions at passing students.

"Aren't you meant to wait until you've done your speech?" Putu asks, seeing me hand out the papers.

Michelle Kadarusman

'Yes, you're right," I agree. "It's nerves."

"Do you want me to hold your hand?" Putu asks.

"Yes," I admit. "But just until we get to the classroom."

Putu takes my hand and squeezes it. "You'll be great, just breathe."

Ginger Juice

Rain *tap, tap, tap* **on** hand and then inside head. It make me remember. I always try hide before-life behind haze. Keep it safe. But this day, rain scent make me remember.

Calls me to before-life inside hum and chatter of jungle. *Croaking, buzzing, thrashing, whirring* sounds of home, safe in treetops. There me and you, Ibu, we wake up in soft nest high above forest floor. In early dawn, *wa-wa-wa* of gibbons make first echo across treetops. Then *whip* and *trill* songbirds, then cackling hornbills. Eyes open to soft *klong, klong, klong* of bamboo stalks nudging each other.

High in jungle home I nestle into you, waiting and

watching. You show me to scoop sweet durian pods from hard, spiky shells. Sun up now, and warm rays dance through canopy. Chattering monkeys rest. And now come hum of cicadas, crickets, and katydids.

You carry heavy durian fruit from low branches back to nest. Bang spiky shell against rough bark. Shell so thick you smash, smash, smash many times against tree trunk.

I put small hand on big hand to help. You nod once, happy for help. Durian fruit crack open, and you show how dig, dig, dig out creamy white fruit with skinny fingers.

I squeeze soft food into mouth, *mmm*, sweet juice drip down to chest. So proud to show you I clever, feed self. I stand up, shrieking, waving small arms in air, *hhk, hhk, hhk!* You stretch mouth in quick smile before settle me down again with strong hands. Back to work, back to work.

Eat, eat, you motion. *This your job now. To eat. Not playtime now.* Every touch, every gaze, every nudge, tell me what you want me do.

Ibu, you always teach me, show me, how to live, how to survive. How to be ape.

Before-life end that day. Durian fruit almost finished when first we hear sound. Bad sound. Big sound. Sound like rumble thunder, so loud shakes ground under treetops. Louder than sky thunder.

You gather me in and look to bad sound. You stay calm and silent, waiting for noise to stop. I stay quiet too, head squeezed under your arm, afraid, waiting for you tell me it safe again.

BERANI

But bad sound does not stop, it grows louder, louder. We cannot hear other forest animals, only screeching roar of big thunder.

Smell of forest changes that day too. Air hangs with bitter, rotten smell. Scent I now know is smell of human.

You hold me tighter and tighter to your strong body. You stop. You think, think. *Stay or go? Stay or go?* I cling to you, trust, believe you know best to do, because you always do. You my Ibu. My mother.

Then bad sound stops. Fast, fast turns to something else. Something that makes us even more afraid. Like forest screaming. Cracking sounds as giant treetops go *crash, crash, crash* to ground.

Durian shell falls from nest when you throw me on your back. I hold on tight because now we are going to move. Swing, swing, swing! When you move us, you move us *fast*. Swing branch to branch through canopy, you know vines that hold our weight, move us quick, quick through jungle.

But no matter how far we swing from tree to tree, we cannot get away.

One, two, three, many, many giants fall, smashing to ground. You climb higher and higher into canopy, swing from branch to branch, trying to escape.

We find safe place in trunk of dark red meranti tree. We crouch there. Almost dusk when forest screaming stops, but quiet does not bring peace. Quiet carries something else.

Quiet carries bigger fear—*fire!*

Ari

Yosef does not mince words on the bus journey to our opponents' private school. The journey from Malang to Surabaya will take a little over an hour.

"Lucky break for you, Ari," he says. "Try not to embarrass us."

"No, Sir," I answer. The *sir* is maybe overdoing it considering Yosef is only two years older than me, but better to pad my good fortune under the circumstances. I am rewarded with a small nod from Yosef.

Faisel nudges me. "There is prize money, you know."

"Seriously?" I ask.

Michelle Kadarusman

"Yep. The school gets a trophy and the ultimate winning player takes home the big money prize."

"How much?" I ask, and Faisel tells me a number that gets my heart racing. I ask him to repeat himself because I can hardly believe my ears.

We arrive at the school reception and tell them who we are. "You will be given a student escort to take you to the games room," the office administrator tells us. "You can sit over there until they come for you."

Our assigned escort arrives ten minutes later. A boy wearing a dark blue blazer with his school logo on the chest pocket extends his hand to me in greeting. "Welcome to SMP," he says. "I'll take you to the games room. The matches will start soon." He opens the door of the office and motions for us to go ahead. Another doorway leads to a covered walkway. The gardens are beautifully manicured, and students stand around talking.

The difference between this private school and our public school is obvious in the amount of space they have. At our school you can't walk in the halls without bumping shoulders with other students. Here the wide walkways and gardens give a glimpse of a much different experience. It hints at a life with the luxury of space and beauty.

I can't help but slow my step as two girls, one tall, the other shorter, walk determinedly toward me. I lock eyes with the taller girl. Hers are alight with an inner glow, a rare kind of illumination and color I have never seen. Something like amber. Or cola over ice. I am struck, momentarily speechless.

40

She thrusts a piece of paper into my hand with no word of explanation and without breaking her swift stride.

"Who...who is that?" I ask, gripping the paper.

Our escort looks behind us as the girls disappear through the door we have just come through. "That's Malia. She's mixed. Mother *bule*, father *orang asli*. You'll be smart not to get in her way. She is very bossy."

I look at the paper she has handed me. It appears to be some kind of petition. The text blurs on the page; I can't quite make it out without my glasses. I put the paper away in my satchel. *Now is not the time to get distracted,* I warn myself. *You must keep focused on the game.*

The rules of the tournament are explained to us. It will be run in the Swiss format with each player completing seven games. Each game is scored with a point for a win, half a point for a tie, and zero for a loss. The top four scoring teams will go on to the semifinals. My first opponent is a boy named Hendra. He opens strong, developing his minor pieces early and taking possession of the center of the board. But twenty moves in, he makes the fatal error of leaving his king vulnerable, and I checkmate him with my rook. Hendra at first looks shocked but is quick with a sportsmanly handshake of congratulations. He smiles. "You caught me with my guard down. Well played."

His fellow students also congratulate me and are all good-natured about the loss. These affluent players do not care so much about the tournament, I see now. They don't care about the prize money and are not hungry for the win.

My circumstances have oddly put me at an advantage, one that I will not lose sight of.

At the end of the afternoon I have won five of my seven games, and our team has qualified for the regional semifinals. Even Yosef is smiling. "You did well for your first tournament," he says as we board the bus home. I grin, taking my seat next to Faisel.

"Faisel has guided my game well," I say, giving him a pat on his shoulder.

"The student has surpassed the teacher," says Faisel. He finished the day with only three wins.

"Not true," I say. "I just had a lucky round." But both Faisel and Yosef are looking at me differently, and it feels good—like I have stepped into a beam of golden light.

It's a warm glow that I won't ever forget.

Malia

My classmates remain silent as I finish my speech. I am frozen to the spot but manage to nod at Putu to dim the lights. I start the Greenpeace video, *Rang-Tan*. It's a lively animated short film depicting a young girl who has an unwelcome guest in her bedroom. Rang-Tan makes a mess of the girl's room and howls at items that contain palm oil, such as chocolate and shampoo. Then Rang-Tan tells the girl why he has nowhere to sleep. The video shows real images of bulldozers and fire destroying the forests to make way for palm oil plantations. The video ends with the words *Dedicated to the twenty-five orangutans we lose every* *day. Let's stop palm oil from destroying the rain forest. Sign the petition.*

The class erupts into applause as Putu turns the lights back on.

"I have created my own petition to protest the government banning products from our supermarket that display palm-free labels," I say, loudly enough for them to hear above the clapping. I wave the paper petition above my head. "I've also created an online form that I will post to our class Web page." I pause and survey the room as the noise subsides. "We, as consumers, need to choose products that we know are not harming the orangutans, and without these labels we can't be properly informed."

The students rush at me to grab a copy of the petition, and I am suddenly surrounded by faces congratulating me and patting me on the back. "I have also included information about orangutan organizations that rehabilitate animals that have been held in captivity. It is illegal to keep an orangutan as a pet...." My voice has been drowned out by the chatter of the students. I kick myself for forgetting this part of the speech, but allow myself a small smile. My presentation has been a success. Everyone wants to sign the form.

I notice our teacher Mrs. Harwono is frowning at a copy of the petition someone has given her. She motions to Putu to turn the lights off again.

"Quiet please, class," she says. "Go back to your seats." The students do as they are told, and once everyone is seated Mrs. Harwono restores the lights. "Malia, you can sit down as well," she tells me. Mrs. Harwono is still frowning, which is unlike her. She places the petition on her desk. "I'm sorry, class, but you will all have to leave Malia's petition here. I need to get permission from the school principal before this is circulated."

The students groan but don't protest as Mrs. Harwono moves around the room gathering the papers. The elation that flooded me a moment ago has just as quickly drained away. I remember my broken promise to Mom, about telling the teacher about my petition before the presentation.

"We will speak after class," Mrs. Harwono says to me, taking the remainder of the petitions from my hand.

"This is a complicated subject, Malia. It is not as simple as it appears," Mrs. Harwono says once class is over. "I know your intentions are good, but I cannot allow a petition to go home with the students without permission from the principal. Especially as the school name is included."

"But it's not fair what is happening to the forests and the orangutans. Why can't we protest? What does it have to do with the school?"

"You must understand that what the students do reflects on our school. Many parents in our community are involved in agriculture and various levels of government. What you are doing might inflame some of these people. I am not saying you do not have a right to protest. You do. But circulating a petition that involves the school—this must first be approved by the principal."

"But he won't approve it, will he?"

"Probably not," she admits. "But I will try. I promise I will try."

She pats my hand. "I want you to know that I admire your convictions, I truly do. But there are rules we must follow here. This is not Canada."

Her comment stings. "I know where we are," I say, unable to keep the anger from my voice. "I am Indonesian."

"I didn't mean to offend you, Malia. I just meant to say that we don't have the same freedoms of expression here in Indonesia that are normal in other countries, such as Canada." She smiles. I can tell she wants to try and make light of what she has said. "Your mother will explain better, I'm sure."

It doesn't matter that I speak Bahasa and attend an Indonesian school. My lighter skin, my white mother, everyone still paints me as an outsider. Even Mrs. Harwono, who I like a lot, still sees me as bule, a foreigner.

"I will make an appointment to meet with Mr. Ahmad, the principal, and I promise I will let you know as soon as he makes a decision," she says. "OK?"

"OK," I say.

"Until then, you are not permitted to give out any of these to students, do you understand?" she asks, holding the petitions aloft.

I nod, wondering if I should tell her about the few petitions I handed out on the way to class. I decide not to. After all, I didn't know then that I wasn't allowed to give them out. Besides, I have already decided what I'll do when I get home.

BERANI

I will post the online petition that I've already set up on the class Web page. Technically, I have not lied. I only promised not to give out the paper version.

Real activists don't let rules get in their way.

Putu is waiting for me outside the classroom. I don't tell her my plan about the online petition. Even the hint of breaking a rule makes her nervous. "What happened?" she asks.

"I promised to do what I'm told," I tell her.

Putu looks at me sideways but doesn't say anything.

It occurs to me that Putu has been oddly silent about the threat of my moving to Canada. I would expect her to be outraged at the prospect of me leaving, but she is not. Am I a burden as a friend, with my irritability and bad temper? I have always suspected that one day Putu would want to step out of my shadow. Maybe she sees this as her chance.

I decide to interrogate her on the way to our next class.

"Do you want me to move?" I ask her. "Tell me honestly."

"You sound like you're accusing me of something. You have to move because of your mother. It's not my fault."

"Yes, but do you *want* me to go, is what I am asking."

"Of course, I don't *want* you to go," she says. "But...but I do think it is your duty to support your mother and...and..." she stops.

"Go on," I badger her. "Spill it."

"You are lucky to have the opportunity to live in Canada, to live and study abroad...and you don't appreciate your good fortune."

"You think I'm a spoiled brat," I say.

"Yes," says Putu kindly. "But don't worry," she adds. "I will come and visit you, and we will go *bobby-saying*." She says the last two words in English.

"You mean bob sleighing, but nobody calls it that. It's called tobogganing."

"No," says Putu. "You're trying to fool me. Who would make up such a strange word?" She eyes me suspiciously, and I wonder how I could ever live without her.

Ari

On the bus ride home, I am as light as air.

I replay my wins over and over in my mind and smile with each recollected checkmate. Then I remember the striking girl who thrust a paper into my hand. I put on my glasses and find the crumpled paper in my satchel. I scan it quickly and see that it is a petition asking for signatures to protest the banning of palm-free labeled products in supermarkets. It also explains the damage palm oil agriculture has caused to orangutans and their habitat.

I think instantly of Ginger Juice, of course, and feel glad that we at least are able to keep her safely away from the described forest destruction. There is a Web site and password to sign the petition, and I promise myself I will do so the next time I have access to a computer at the Internet Café. Or, as instructed on the petition, I could mail this paper directly to the address included. The intensity of the girl's eyes will not leave me, and I'm drawn to sign it for her. Before I put the paper away, I read on and see a box of text:

> KEEPING ORANGUTANS AS PETS IS AGAINST THE LAW. IF YOU KNOW OF ONE BEING HELD IN CAPTIVITY, YOU SHOULD CALL AUTHORITIES. CAPTIVE ORANGUTANS CAN BE RESCUED AND SENT TO REHABILITATION CENTERS WHERE THEY CAN LIVE IN CONDITIONS MORE LIKE THEIR NATURAL ENVIRONMENT. SOMETIMES THEY CAN BE RETURNED TO THE WILD. WITH SO FEW WILD ORANGUTANS LEFT, EVERY CAPTIVE ORANGUTAN IS IMPORTANT. DON'T REMAIN SILENT IF YOU CAN HELP A CAPTIVE ORANGUTAN.

Reading the text stops my breath for a few seconds. It's like the girl has personally reached into my chest and squeezed my heart. Surely this does not apply to Ginger Juice?! She is loved and adored with us. We keep her safe from the harm that could befall her in the jungle. I crunch up the paper and stuff it into my satchel. Clearly this girl is not properly informed. Her petition won't get my signature after all.

BERANI

I look out of the bus window and watch the congested streets of Surabaya give way to patches of green. Snatches of rice paddies can be seen beyond the roadside *satay* stalls and snack vendors as we climb closer to Malang. The warm glow of elation I had enjoyed from winning the tournament is gone.

Malia

After school I go to sit under the mango tree. The earth is moist and spongy under its heavy branches, but the rain has finally stopped. Leaves float lazily to the ground in the warm, damp air. I breathe in the scent of the tuberoses that cover the cemetery and brush dead petals from Papa's gravestone. I try to complain to Papa about leaving Indonesia, but it doesn't help at all. Papa loved Canada. On our yearly visits to Mom's family's lakeside cottage, he became a full-fledged Canadian. He walked around wearing a Blue Jays baseball cap and a Raptors basketball T-shirt. He watched the hockey games that my uncles taped for him. "It's hard to be a Maple Leaf's fan," he would lament. "But they'll take it next year for sure." Forever the optimist.

He even swam in the lake every day, which was far too cold for me. "Maple syrup in my veins!" he would shout to us proudly as he bobbed around not far from the shore. He spent his time by the lake doing all the activities that he never did growing up in Surabaya. He made campfires and took canoe trips. He hiked in the woods and went on fishing expeditions with the uncles. The cottage was an exotic place for him. So, as I sit and try to complain about moving to Toronto, all I can hear him saying is "All that fresh air and clean water. Free healthcare and education. Yes, it's a terrible, terrible place."

Papa could be what Canadians call a real *smart aleck*.

My mom, on the other hand, is more what you would call a straight shooter. She is tall and athletic with light brown hair and hazel eyes. She grew up playing hockey with her two older brothers, who say they didn't cut her any slack for being a girl. She is fun and seriously fearless. I've watched her surf and scuba dive and bungee jump. One time at the cottage my grandfather said he thought he'd heard a bear by the garbage bins, and it was Mom who went outside, banging two pots together and yelling at it to go away. We all stayed inside watching her from the window. She is quick to smile and she is very, very kind. She is forever going out of her way to help her graduate students with foreign visa applications and academic recommendations. But she also has a stubborn streak. If you try to push her, you will come up hard against a brick wall. "Strong-willed" is how Papa described her. What he would actually say was "You are every bit as strong-willed as your mother." He'd usually say this to me after Mom and I had had an argument.

Growing up, I was painfully aware of how different Mom was from all of the other petite, soft-spoken, Indonesian mothers. She stood out in every way, and I was ashamed. Not of her exactly, but I was ashamed of being different. I hated explaining where she was from and then trying to disqualify the "otherness" in myself by saying "But I was born here, I am Indonesian." I still feel shame for feeling shame. But there are also times when I've felt the undeserved pride that comes with being connected to Western culture. American movies and television shows are popular in Indonesia, and people sometimes confuse Canada and America.

My parents met at the University of Toronto where Papa was doing his PhD in bioethics and Mom was doing her master's degree in linguistic studies, specializing in Asian languages. She was learning to speak Bahasa, so when someone told her about my dad being at the university, she sent him an e-mail asking if she could take him out for coffee to practice her conversational skills. The coffee date turned into happily ever after. Papa would joke that Mom never stopped practicing her conversational skills on him, and Mom says she knew she'd nailed the language when she managed to win an argument with him in Bahasa.

The truth is, it was always my parents' plan for us to move back to Toronto after I finished elementary school. I've always known this. I was always meant to start middle school in Toronto. It's even possible that Papa was looking forward to the move more than Mom. What wasn't in the plan was Papa getting sick.

It was never the plan to move there without him.

My thoughts are broken when I see that Oma, my grand-mother, is standing in front of me with a bunch of roses in her arms. She is wearing large designer sunglasses, a silk headscarf, and a tailored suit. She places the flowers on Papa's grave and tucks a loose strand of hair behind my ear.

"Always so messy, this hair of yours," she says.

It is her way of saying I would look neater, more accept-able, if I wore a headscarf. Oma likes to begin our conversations with a criticism. She thinks it is character building. I ignore her comment about my hair and stand up to properly greet her. Our hands clasp and our cheeks touch, once each side.

"Hello, Oma," I say. "I didn't know you were coming today."

"Only for a moment to place fresh flowers on my son's grave." Her shoulders slump slightly as she looks at Papa's headstone. "Then I have a business meeting," she says, straight-ening. "Do you want a ride home?"

"No, it's OK, I feel like walking."

Oma takes off her sunglasses and studies my face. "How is school?" she asks. "Is everything all right?"

"School is fine," I say, remembering the online petition I want to send out to my class. "Actually, I will grab a ride after all."

Oma shakes her head and makes a *tsk-tsk* sound. "Come on then, before you change your mind again."

She reaches for my arm and leans on it for balance. It reminds me that she is an old woman—a fact that always surprises me. Her high heels stick in the soft, wet earth, making squelching noises as we walk to her Mercedes.

Oma grips my hand tightly, and I know she's grateful to have me close. It is still difficult for her to accept Papa's death. It is difficult for all of us.

Ari

Uncle owns a transistor radio that he is very proud of. He cleans it regularly and tells me it never lets him down. *Dangdut* music crackles from it on the nights when his friends come over to play dominoes. They often play late into the night. The restaurant tables are dragged into a large square with enough places for all the players. Muslim men are not permitted to gamble, so Uncle assures anyone who asks that the games are just for fun, for sport. I know very well that betting is included, but his friends are mostly army personnel, so no one dares challenge them.

That is how Uncle came to own Ginger Juice. She was

offered as winnings by a player, a commander at the local army base, who gave her in lieu of the cash he owed. Uncle said he knew a bargain when he saw one. Baby orangutans can fetch a much higher price than what he was owed. Originally, he intended to sell her to make a profit, but he ended up getting attached to her.

We all did.

When she was little, she used to love to do somersaults on the grass and climb the trunk of a date palm in the garden. As children, we would tickle her to hear her deep throaty laugh, a *hhk, hhk* sound that never failed to charm us. We treated her like our little cousin, carrying her on our hips and even taking her for car rides to visit other relatives.

At first, the cage was only a place to put her when she'd have temper tantrums, throwing things or refusing to come down from the roof. Uncle became afraid she would run away. Another army pal gave him a cage, explaining it had once held a baby Sumatran tiger. The fate of the tiger and why it no longer required the cage was never explained. Uncle told us keeping Ginger Juice in the cage was for her own benefit, to keep her safe in the evenings. But the restaurant patrons soon enjoyed watching her in her cage, so she became an attraction instead of a beloved pet.

This morning as I hose out her enclosure, I can't help but remember what I read on the girl's petition. It prompts me to look at the cage with new eyes, and I have to admit that the space has become woefully too small for her. When she was little, she could climb and hang from the bars, but now her size no longer gives her the room to do either.

I switch off the hose. "A larger enclosure is what you need," I tell her. It is the first time I have spoken to her in a very long time, I realize. Does she remember how we used to play together? The idea fills me with nostalgia and before I think about what I am doing, I reach through the bars and lightly stroke her arm. In response, Ginger Juice slowly reaches toward me and my hand disappears in the fold of her huge hand. Palm to palm, we sit together in silence. I am mutely in awe of what is happening. Her grasp is enormous, but her grip is gentle and comforting. *How long has it been since she has been touched?* I wonder. I look into her soft eyes and see only gentleness.

Yes, this is the answer, I think to myself, mesmerized by her gaze. *She just needs a cage large enough so she can climb like she used to. And perhaps some activities. When she was little, she loved to play with soccer balls. I could easily get her some balls to play with once she has a large enough area to tumble around in.* I resolve to talk to Uncle about this and I dismiss again what I've read on the girl's petition.

Ginger Juice belongs with us, that is certain.

Malia

Before I go to bed, I open my computer to check the online petition I uploaded to the class Web page a few hours ago. It's Friday night, with plenty of time over the weekend for students to sign the form and e-mail it directly to the government office at the Drug and Food Control Agency. I had sourced their e-mail contact and included it on the petition. This is the government arm that issued the directive to ban "anti-palm" products. And because it's the weekend, Mrs. Harwono likely won't see it. Not until Monday.

Before I go onto the class Web page, I log in to my e-mail. There is an e-mail in my inbox titled: *Hey Bule!* The e-mail itself has no other content apart from the title, and the sender's address is made up of numbers, no name.

I'm used to being called bule. I'm different, not just my foreign mother, but I'm not Muslim either. My not being Muslim is a subject that causes some upset in my Indonesian family and a rift between Mama and Oma. Oma would like me to be a Muslim girl like the rest of her family.

"If you want to belong to a religion, it is up to you. You can choose it yourself when you are old enough to decide," is what Mom says when I ask her about it. I should wait until I am grown up as far as she's concerned. This is an unusual view of religion compared to those of my friends' parents, for whom religion is highly important. Mom was raised Christian but no longer practices the faith. Papa was raised Muslim but observed only, it seemed, for the benefit of Oma. She would chide him if he did not fast during Ramadan, or if he missed Friday prayers. His travel and work commitments were always his excuse. Maybe because my parents came from such different cultures, they chose to be neutral when it came to religion.

When Papa was alive, the three of us would hold our arms next to each other and say "Chocolate, mocha, and vanilla!" As a little girl, that's how I would explain myself, being bi-racial, as an ice-cream flavor. I've met other *campuran*, mixed-race kids, of course. Mom has always had plenty of friends who are also foreigners married to Indonesians, but their kids go to international schools. None of the campuran kids I've met identify as Indonesian like I do.

Anyway, being called bule is nothing new to me. I delete the e-mail.

I close my laptop and put it on my bedside table, turn off my lamp, and close my eyes. A flutter of panic sparks behind my eyelids. Part of me can't believe that I have circulated the petition after being explicitly told not to. A combination of fear and excitement swims up and down my body. This is what it feels like to take action instead of just talking. This is what it feels like to be a real activist.

When I wake up the next morning, I check the class Web page. My petition has been clicked on twenty-three times. I keep checking over the course of the weekend. The number continues to grow and grow. By Sunday morning the click count is one hundred and twenty-three. This means students from my class have sent the petition to others.

Putu texts me a series of emojis to illustrate the success of the petition each time she checks the click count. Once I explained the online petition "loophole" she felt secure enough to be a cheerleader for the undercover project. Plus, she can rest easy in the added security of being away. She is in Bali for the weekend with her parents attending an older relative's cremation. The Hindu cremation ceremony is a huge event for Balinese families, and no expense is spared. It's a festival to celebrate the deceased and a chance to set them free from earthly ties. It has to be done properly so that the loved one can enter the eternal world. There are long processions that stop local traffic for hours at a time. Putu sent me photos so I could see her in traditional dress. She looks like a princess with gold sashes around her waist and orange flowers in her hair.

On Sunday afternoon she dispenses with the emojis and texts VIRAL.

I smile to myself, imagining the tsunami of e-mails the government agency will receive on Monday morning.

Ari

To succeed in chess, you must learn to plan many steps ahead of your next move. It is said that chess masters play ten moves ahead. Much like a chess player, I decide to strategize before broaching the subject of improving Ginger Juice's enclosure with Uncle. Not being able to afford the improvements myself, it will be necessary to convince him to spend money, which will be something of a miracle.

Just like an advanced player, I plan my opening move, then counter moves depending on his predicted responses. *The trick*, I remind myself, *is to keep ahead of the play and to be prepared for various options.* Once I am sufficiently armed with supporting arguments—The restaurant patrons will enjoy seeing Ginger Juice more active, for example—I go to the restaurant kitchen in search of Uncle. Better to approach him when he is busy with another task as he is more likely to be agreeable. This is a strategy I have successfully adopted in the past. But the kitchen only holds Nang, his cook helper. She is peeling and slicing potatoes for the soup. A growing mound of peel sits at her feet as she deftly slices potatoes into an enormous pink plastic bowl.

"He is gone for fried rice," she says, not taking her eyes from her work. "He won't be back till later." She glances at me to see if I have understood. I have. She means he won't be back until *much* later.

It seems odd, but Uncle does not eat his own speciality. Sop buntut gives him gas, he says. As his housemate, I can only be grateful that he buys *nasi goreng* instead at a nearby food stall, a local hangout. He loves his food, Uncle does. He orders double portions and uses a rice ladle instead of a spoon so he can really shovel it in. He always grins when he eats.

For me there is steamed white rice and the remnants of the daily soup pot left over from the day's sales. Often the day-old rice is a bit crispy and dry, but with plenty of the soup's rich broth it makes for a flavorful meal. Not much of the oxtail remains at the end of the day, but there's plenty of carrot and onion.

I fix myself a bowl and allow my mind to wander as I eat. It fills itself with thoughts of the tournament prize money. *What I could do with such a windfall!*

BERANI

But soon the many options begin to circle my head like a merry-go-round. The obvious choice of giving the money to my parents, of course, is at the top of the list. And the notion of buying a large gift for Suni hovers. Something truly wonderful that might help to chip away at my boulder of guilt. Thoughts of buying myself a laptop or phone shine brightly as well. And then there is Ginger Juice, of course. I could use the money to build her a bigger enclosure myself.

My mind rattles with the possibilities, and I am almost relieved to remember that no decision is necessary. I have no money and I have not won the tournament.

But you might, a little voice whispers. *You just might.*

Malia

"**Oh, boy, do you have** some explaining to do."

Mom is in my bedroom, and it's still dark. She has risen even earlier than Bibi. I sit up and squint from the light she has turned on. "What are you talking about?" I ask, but I know exactly what she is talking about.

"Your online petition. I have twenty-seven e-mails. Twenty-seven! All from parents and teachers at your school." She is furious. "Malia, you promised me you would ask your teacher before you gave out the petition."

I nod. "I know I did," I admit. "But the presentation went so well, and all of the students were so excited to sign it." I rub my eyes. "Mrs. Harwono said I couldn't give out the paper version until she spoke with the principal but she didn't say anything about the online petition. What kind of activist would I be if I didn't find a way to galvanize support?" I had read that phrase on a blog somewhere.

"Oh, come on, Malia! You know very well what she meant." Mom shakes her head. "I am so disappointed in you. I just can't believe you would do such a thing, directly disobey both your teacher and me in this way."

"It's not that much of a big deal, is it?" I ask her. "I mean it's just a petition. Why are you so upset?"

"Because I've just been speaking on the phone with Mrs. Harwono and..."

"And what?" I sit up.

"You *and* Mrs. Harwono have been suspended from school until they can look further into the matter."

The force of the word *suspended* flattens me back onto my pillow. I remember my conversation with Mrs. Harwono and how I felt when she said "This is not Canada." *Did I send the online petition to get back at her? To punish her?* I push the unwelcome thought away.

"But it's not her fault, why would they suspend Mrs. Harwono? That's not fair. She didn't know anything about the online petition," I say.

"No, it isn't fair," Mom says. "This could have very serious repercussions for her." *And it's your fault.* Mom doesn't say the words, but they drift in the air between us. She sits on my bed. "Depending on what happens, this might mean we leave for

Canada earlier than expected. You're enrolled to start middle school in Toronto in September. This term is extra for you anyway because the Indonesian system begins in January." She sighs. "But that's beside the point. What has happened is serious, Malia. We have to clear Mrs. Harwono from any wrongdoing. She is a good teacher and a good person. She does not deserve this."

No. No. No. Everything is unraveling in the wrong direction. This is not going according to plan at all.

"But I don't want to go to Canada!" I say thumping the mattress. "I'm not going to leave Oma, or Putu, or Bibi. And what about Bibi anyway?" I throw at her, trying to change the subject. "We can't just abandon her!"

"Not this again, Malia. We've been over this too many times already. I'm not in the mood to repeat the argument." Her voice is detached and calm. Too calm. "You know that Oma is already planning to visit us in Toronto. And you will come back and stay with her for holidays. And as for Bibi, she is looking forward to her retirement. She's an old woman. Don't you think she deserves to stop working?"

The idea of Bibi not wanting to be here taking care of us has never occurred to me. The idea of her looking forward to us leaving feels...impossible. I put this notion away as well, not wanting to lose sight of my argument.

"How many times do I have to tell you, I am Indonesian," I say. "I want to say in Indonesia."

"You're half Canadian too, remember?" she says.

"But what does that mean, *half*? Half my brain? Half my

heart? Half my body? What if I never feel *half* Canadian? What if I never do, even after I've lived there for years and years? What if I always feel wholly Indonesian?"

"There aren't any answers to these questions, Malia. The answers you are looking for can't be told, they are yours, and yours only, to explore and find out." Mom sighs. "Look. I know this is hard. I know you miss your dad. I do too."

For a horrible moment I think she might begin to cry. I silently kick myself for edging her back into the forbidden zone. We are so much better now. Images of Mom flash in my mind. Of her mute with grief after Papa died, of her unable to eat or sleep. Of countless days, then months, of her not leaving her room. Endless tears. And then, slowly, slowly of her clawing her way back to herself. Back to life again—for me.

"But right now," she goes on, rallying herself much to my relief, "you are not going to distract me from this petition."

I swing my legs out of bed. "I'll get dressed," I tell her. "I will fix this, I promise."

Ginger Juice

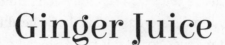

Slow Loris Boy is talking, but I not want to learn human words anymore.

Long ago I want to learn because humans might teach me things. Teach me things like you teach me, Ibu. Like what reed best to chew for make strong teeth and what leaf hold rainwater best.

I learn human word for this place that holds me. Call it *cage*. And strong sticks that hold me inside, call it *bars*. I learn *no*, I learn *bad*.

I learn *good* and *gentle*.

But human words give me no use.

Humans do not try understand ape language. Cannot make them understand me. They do not see when I try show them name. Name you give me. And I never make humans understand how much I want go home. Back to you, Ibu.

But I feel comfort from human gentle touch. Surprise to feel warmth inside me. Has been long, long time to feel this warm feeling. It pulls more thinking inside head from before-life, when not in cage. Not in this place where I cannot stretch or climb or walk.

But I glad Slow Loris Boy not afraid anymore. Tried to tell him with eyes not to be afraid. I know how afraid feels.

After fire we have only small patch of forest left. We do not know where gibbons, macaques, or apes go. You sing across treetops. Other apes used to sing to us before fire. But not now.

After fire, no apes return your songs, Ibu.

Our small patch of trees gives not enough to eat, so you go to the dangerous place to find food. That is what you call it. *It is a dangerous place where I go, you must stay here. Stay in nest until I come back.*

Feel afraid when you leave me in nest all alone.

I scared Thunder Beast will come back to smash down tree nest. Or Fire Monster come back to burn me. But I know you come back, Ibu. Mothers always take care of baby. That is our way. That is ape way.

So, I stay in nest and wait. Forest sounds all gone. No life in our little patch of trees. Even the gentle *klong, klong, klong* of bamboo stalks—gone. All burned and gone. *Buzz, buzz, buzz* of cicadas, crickets, and katydids are only song, so me hum along to insect music.

When you come back, you have not much from your long, long time away. One banana, maybe two, and strange sticks of food with bright-color peel that cannot be chewed. Inside the strange sticks is very salty. Very, very sticky and so sweeeeet, sweet, sweet. I love sweet.

But strange food sticks do not fill our bellies, and make us thirsty instead. In before-life, we drink juice from different fruits and rain that sits on the big leaves. But not now.

Now, me and you weak from hunger and thirst. You look around many times, try to find a safe place and food, but see only burned ground around our trees.

When you know we cannot live like this, you take me with you to the dangerous place. *You must learn get food from this place,* you tell me. *We have no food now. You must learn how do this.*

I happy at first because this means not have to be in the nest alone for long, long time while you search for food. You are tense and alert now. You do not play with me anymore and you do not laugh or smile like you used to. When cuddle into you, your body is thin, skin is loose.

I learn, I promise. *I brave, just like you, Ibu,* I tell you.

First time we go to dangerous place, I cling to your back and keep chin high, want to make you proud.

We climb down from the treetops at early dawn, all the way down to ground!

Tree apes never put feet on ground. Being on ground makes

us afraid because ground is not where we are safe. Our safe place is in treetops.

I feel your heart pound faster, faster as we move along the forest floor, and my heart follows like smaller drumbeat. We leave safe cover of forest. Cool shade of leaves gives way to burned ground left by fire. Black. Char. Ash.

From perch on your back I see dead ground. No more life. No more forest. No more birds, butterflies, lizards, bugs, monkeys. No more apes.

We walk for long time in the burning sun. I not used to the heat of sun outside of treetop canopy. *We are coming to the dangerous place now*, you say. *Do not let go.*

I cling tighter to you, forget my brave feelings.

First thing I see as you walk us into the danger place is *food!* You bring us to big human food place. Much, much fruit, durians, papayas, rambutans, and bananas. My belly growls for this fruit.

We must be quick now, you say. *Before humans can catch us. Ibu will take what can carry and we will go back to the forest.* You grab at handfuls of fruit. I want to grab some too, but you tell me *Hold tight!* So I hold with both arms as tight, tight as can.

It is there I see human for first time. On that day I think it is tall, hairless ape, walking upright, with strange-colored skin instead of hair. It run at us, waving large stick and yelling language we do not know, but me and you understand meaning good enough.

Go away, go away, go away, or will hurt you!

Ari

I am determined to be strong and confident in my plea to Uncle, but my first attempt is shot down fast. I finally approach him when he returns from the warung and is preparing the tables for the evening domino game. Dangdut music crackles from the transistor radio.

"A what?" he asks. "For who?"

"A large enclosure!" I repeat with a flourish of my hands to try and indicate its grandeur. "For Ginger Juice, so she can roll and play and climb as she used to do."

Uncle snorts. "Why? She is grown up now, she doesn't need this. And who will pay for it?"

"It would be an investment...." I falter before remembering my counter arguments. "Your patrons would see you as very generous and successful." Uncle's chest puffs for a moment before he waves the thought away.

"Too expensive," he says. "She is not a baby anymore. She doesn't need to play."

"But think of her well-being," I plead. "It isn't only baby orangutans that need activity."

"Enough of this talk," he says irritably. "I don't want to hear about it again. She has a perfectly good cage. Just keep it clean, like I told you to." He glances toward Ginger Juice. "The only thing she needs to is be fed and kept clean."

"But, but..." Uncle's glower stops me from bombarding him with more supporting arguments.

"Don't you still have today's accounts to do?" he asks. "Don't try my patience any longer, boy." He takes hold of one of the tables and gestures for me to take the other end. "Here. Help me set these up first and then go and do the books."

I obey him, of course. The injustice to Ginger Juice stirs in my gut causing me to huff and puff, which Uncle probably thinks is due to the exertion of arranging the furniture.

Once we have the game tables set up, and before tackling the accounts, I go back to talk to Ginger Juice. Now that I have started a conversation with her, I feel it's only fair to tell her the outcome.

Or maybe it is because I want to feel the touch of her huge warm hand enveloping mine once again.

I find a group of young children surrounding her cage

throwing peanuts at her. I recognize the children from around the neighborhood.

"Hey, stop that!" I shout. The giggling children ignore me and continue to throw peanuts at Ginger Juice. She is lying on her stomach, facing away from the restaurant with her head resting on crossed arms. Being pelted with peanuts does nothing to rouse her.

"We want to wake her up!" one of them says. "She is so lazy."

"She's not lazy," I say, grabbing at the bag of peanuts to make them stop. "She's just..." *She's what?* I wonder to myself. "...she's just sleeping," I say finally.

"She's always sleeping," the children whine. "We want her to play with us."

"Go home," I say, thrusting the bag of peanuts back at them. "She doesn't want to play now. She's not here for you to play with whenever you feel like it."

"Why is she here then?" one of them asks, throwing one final peanut.

"Go home!" I shout. "And don't come back."

The children finally scatter, one of them turning to pull a face at me before they all scurry away.

Malia

Mom stands over my shoulder as I log onto the class Web page. I want to take down the petition form, but it's not necessary because the school has already deleted it. Not before over two hundred e-mails were sent to the official inbox of the government agency, though.

"This is why the school is reacting this way," Mom's friend Hadi says. "The local government will be telling your principal that this kind of anti-palm oil propaganda has *consequences*." Hadi is a colleague of Mom's from the university where she works. He specializes in governance, so Mom asked for his help. "I have a PhD in red tape," he tells me with a warm smile.

My stomach lurches at the word consequences. "Like, what kind of consequences?" I ask tentatively.

"*Hmm*. Without a public apology from the school, they will likely threaten its license. Yours is a private school, so it is a business that requires licensing. The government does not tolerate media that is not in line with their pro-palm oil propaganda. Palm oil is a sixty-billion-dollar industry. That's why they won't allow any anti-palm oil products in the grocery stores. Simply labeling a product as palm oil free immediately infers that palm oil is bad."

"But it *is* bad!" I say, throwing up my hands.

"Well, that depends on who you are. Palm oil is indeed bad if you are an orangutan, or any other creature living in rainforests that are destroyed in order to plant palm oil plantations. But it isn't bad if you are wanting to sustain a multi-billion-dollar export product."

"It's not fair," I say.

"What is not fair," Mom says, pointedly, "is that Mrs. Harwono might lose her job."

"Don't you care about the orangutans?" I ask her.

"I do, but right now I care more about Mrs. Harwono. If she loses her job over this, the school is unlikely to give her a reference, and without a good reference, she may not be able to find another position. Mrs. Harwono has her husband and children to support."

I remember grimly that Mrs. Harwono's husband was in a car accident last year and has not yet been able to return to his job due to a concussion. We have been trying to get Mrs. Harwono on the telephone all day, but she is not answering our calls. I haven't been able to apologize to her, or find out how I can help keep her job.

"My guess is that your school will be asked to make a public apology, and the statement will declare that the students and staff involved have been reprimanded. Our best hope is that your suspension will suffice as to how the school deals with the punishment.

"It all has to do with public perception. The government is only concerned that their propaganda is supported and upheld publicly. If your school goes along with their wishes, it will all blow over very quickly. It's a storm in a teacup."

"And if they don't cooperate?" I ask.

"Oh, I highly doubt that. Any organization or individual who stands against the explicit wishes of the government faces a very difficult road."

"What if I write an apology to the school saying that Mrs. Harwono had nothing to do with the petition? Will that help?"

"It might help, but what they will want is a statement that says your petition was wrong. Essentially, they'll want you to say that you now understand products with palm oil are not bad and therefore, anti-palm labels are wrong." Hadi searches my face. "Are you willing to do that?"

Before I can respond, my phone rings. It's Putu and she is in tears. The school has been in touch with her parents, and they are on their way back from Bali. The principal, Mr. Ahmad, has summoned her to his office to explain her part in the petition.

"You promised me you weren't doing anything wrong," she

sobs. "What about your loophole?"

My heart breaks at how trusting Putu is of everything I say. I know how terrified she must be at the very idea of speaking with Mr. Ahmad.

"You didn't do anything wrong," I say, trying to calm her. "Don't worry. Just tell him you had nothing to do with it."

"But he will ask if I knew about it," she says. "You know I can't lie."

I remember the texts we exchanged back and forth over the weekend and all of Putu's encouraging emojis.

"I've never been in trouble before," she says quietly. "And we had to leave before my cousin's cremation ceremonies were finished. My parents are so upset."

"I'm sorry," is all I can think of to say. "I'm so sorry."

Ari

All my spare time, what little there is of it, is taken up with preparing for the upcoming chess tournament.

Uncle has been surprisingly supportive since I told him about my qualifying win, even to the extent of buying me a chessboard and a strategy book. He has taken to introducing me to his domino friends as "my nephew the chess master." His army pals see me in a new light and are full of cryptic advice. None of which I can make any sense of at all: *"In chess, he who is willing to commit suicide controls the game."* Or *"Rooks must obey the queen."* I thank them enthusiastically each time.

It is a pleasant feeling to be in Uncle's good favor,

something I haven't felt since I was much younger. Perhaps it is because we now share a common hobby. Even if dominoes is an entirely different game, we have become comrades of a sort.

I have not told him about the prize money.

Now that I have my own chessboard, in the afternoons after the lunch rush, I drag a restaurant table and a chair over to Ginger Juice's cage to practice moves and talk through various strategies with her. She is patient and watches the board and chess pieces with a kind of detached interest as she continues the endless scratching and inspection of her fur. Sometimes I see her eyes following the pieces. At other times she appears to nod in approval or shake her head in warning. Her presence calms my thoughts, and I often find myself reaching through the bars to hold her hand or stroke her foot when I am trying to puzzle out an escape.

Uncle and I have not discussed improving her enclosure again. I am biding my time for another opportunity to present our case.

Faisel and I still meet up at Warung Kopi to play and share strategies. However, in an unspoken agreement, I no longer pay for his coffee and snacks. We are now on equal footing.

The semifinals will be held in two weeks and the finals a week after that. I will be ready.

Yesterday, a letter from Suni arrived. It was so good to see her familiar neat script on the thin blue paper we keep at home for mailing letters. I was eager to read it, even seeing her name on the back of the letter brought a smile. But after reading it, I was left with the familiar gnawing guilt, like a rat chewing on a chicken bone.

Dear Ari,

One of the ducks has disappeared again. It makes me think of the stories we used to make up about what the missing ducks would get up to when they ran off—tea with visiting bird royalty, or a flight to the city to buy a new *sarong*. A duck's life is her own.

How are you, cousin? I know it is selfish of me to wish you would come back for a visit. I know how busy you must be with studies and helping Uncle, but I hope every day to see you walk up our dirt path and ring the ox bell over the front door to announce you are home. Life here is not changed. Except for usual talk from our neighbors about wanting to clear land for more rice paddies. The neighbors are asking our fathers to invest our small savings in their new rice crop. They say it will be a good investment. But how do we know the neighbors won't end up behaving like the wealthy landowners? To be landless, as we are, provides very little security.

Our fathers have spent many nights on the front verandah talking with the neighbors on this subject. I sit with my mother and yours in the living room with the front door open so we can hear the discussions. I'm sure this news will reach Uncle's ears soon enough as they will need his dollars to invest also.

What are your thoughts on this? Do they teach you about crops and farming in school? Our mothers *tsk-tsk* the idea of clearing more forest, saying it will interfere with the quality of water that runs down to our rice paddies. As usual, the men say it is for them to decide.

Selfishly I hope our family can earn more money from rice crops so that I might join you one day at school. It's a silly dream, of course, because even if the fathers decide to invest in the crop, it will take a long time to make profits. But still, it provides a glimmer of hope that our family might have a chance to improve our situation.

Our Uncle tells us that you are now a chess champion! Wah! Congratulations! This doesn't surprise me. You were always so good at *congklak*, the seed-counting game we used to play. Is chess like congklak? How clever you are, my cousin, and how proud we all are of you.

Most evenings I walk to the village and sit with the other girls, so we can watch our nightly television drama at the warung. I like to be with my friends but I find myself growing bored with the storylines. Always so predictable, and the women always so helpless! My mind wanders off, just like the ducks. My girlfriends flap at me for groaning and rolling my eyes every time the dramatic music signals yet another heroic deed by a male character, but I can't help it. It's as if girls dream only of being saved by a handsome boy. Not me.

BERANI

Your mother still makes your favorite dish of rice cakes and vegetables in coconut broth, every Friday. She says it isn't for you, but we know it is. She cranes her neck to look down the path, hoping you might be among the men when they return from the mosque after Friday prayers. I help her to wrap the banana leaves for the rice longtons, and we giggle at our silliness, that the smell of the dish might lure you back, all the way from Malang.

I'm certain that you would wish to know that both of your parents, and mine, are in good health, praise be to Allah. We all pray to Allah for your good health every day, as well.

It is a strange thing to admit, but lately I walk out into the rice paddies after dark when everyone is asleep. The croaking of frogs in the water-filled gullies is so loud that it vibrates the ground under my sandals. The night air moves soft and fragrant from the frangipani trees that line the crops. I lay a sarong over the warm earth and lie down to gaze up at the blanket of stars above. A magical feeling washes over me, looking at the thousands of flickering pinpoints of light. I wonder what is out there in this enormous, wondrous universe. It is a big question for a small person, but I truly believe deep down in my heart that one day I will learn and discover many of the world's mysteries. That one day I might be somebody.

Michelle Kadarusman

Cousin, you are always close in my thoughts, and I write this knowing that you are the only one who will understand my fanciful ideas. Maybe because many of them are those that we shared together as small children. I hope you are in good spirits and you will visit home soon. Give my respectful regards to our uncle. Don't forget to bring your schoolbooks when you come home. I will speed-read them during your much awaited visit!

Your cousin,

Suni

Ginger Juice

I like watch ants. Ants march in long, long line, up, down, in, out of cage. Ants like eating fruits in my cage. Before-life in jungle, we eat tree-ants. Good to have ants in cage. Not alone with them here. So, I not eat cage-ants.

But sometimes I forget. Taste salty.

Slow Loris Boy spends more time near me now. He lost his fear smell now.

He brings a plaything and chatters human words. I don't try understand. He not share his plaything, but I like to watch patterns and colors. What I like best is when Slow Loris Boy holds my hand and I feel smooth skin and beat of another life.

It keep the haze away.

Slow Loris Boy play with me long, long time ago. When I little. Small female human too, who like to carry me. For short time feel comfort with them. It fills hole of missing you, Ibu. But not for long.

This remembering inside head floats and flutters like butterflies past my cage.

After first time you take me to human place, dangerous place, we go many times again. Each time we wait until hunger is angry like wasp nest in our bellies. Then have to leave safety of treetops and go to human place more and more to take their food.

We have nowhere to go and nothing to eat.

You are smaller now, Ibu. You not strong. Can't feed me milk like mother apes give babies. I already eat food, but still want this milk.

After no more milk, then I help snatch food at human place with you. I scamper down from your back and grab at piles of fruit, run back to you fast, fast as can.

You always warn me not to stray. But on day it happen, I go too far.

See *big* papaya, so big it feed us for many days. I shake free from you, want to get big fruit to make you strong again. But when try pick it up, cannot. Papaya too heavy for little ape.

You call me to come back. You shriek warning.

I see you stand up on two feet, watching for me. You hold bananas in one hand, other arm stretch to me. You screaming, *Run fast, fast, fast!* Fear in your scream makes me afraid. Must run fast, fast back to you.

BERANI

Almost there when hear loud *POP, POP, POP*. The noise stops you. One, two, three heartbeats you stand, not moving, with bananas still in hand. Swaying, swaying. Bananas drop. Then you fall. In the dust you fall down.

I jump on you, crying, *Get up. Get up, get up!* See human with long stick running closer and closer. The stick makes more loud *POP, POP, POP* sounds.

Human shouting, waving arms, but I not leave you, Ibu. I try hard to pull your arms, you will not move. Ibu will not get up. You lie very still. Like long, long sleep.

I don't let go of you, even when human hands try pull me loose. Cling to you for as long as small arms can. I bite and scratch at hands that want to take me from you, but humans pull me away.

They put me in cage. Dark in cage, and I very afraid. I cry and cry.

Why they take me from you, Ibu? Where you are? When will you come back for me?

Malia

Everything Mom's friend Hadi predicted was bang on. On the second day of my three-day suspension, the principal asks Mom and me to a meeting to discuss "the unfortunate situation."

As we walk through the school halls, kids stare at us openly. This isn't so unusual. Mom usually turns heads, being as tall and fair as she is, but this time I know the curiosity has to do with me more than her. Seeing a suspended student walking the halls is like seeing a naughty ghost.

We reach the principal's building and are ushered into his office.

"Come and sit down, please," Mr. Ahmad says to Mom in English, motioning to two chairs in front of his desk. He does not make eye contact with me.

Mom answers politely in English. "Thank you, I appreciate your seeing us today."

This is a common dance of language for her. Mom says it can be taken as an insult if she ignores a person's greeting in English, even if it is likely the discussion would be better understood in Bahasa. Often people wish it to be acknowledged to foreigners that they speak English fluently. In this setting, we definitely do not want to offend the principal.

"Of course," he says. "Let me begin by expressing regret for your daughter's suspension. However, it was necessary for us to determine a course of action." He pauses. "I hope you can also appreciate that this has been a very difficult situation for the school." His expression is pained, like he has sucked on a lemon.

"What we are most concerned with is Mrs. Harwono," Mom says. "She is an innocent party in this situation."

"Yes, yes," Mr. Ahmad agrees, but offers no further information about Mrs. Harwono.

"You see," he goes on, "we have friends in the local agricultural administration who have explained to us that Malia has been misinformed about the anti-palm labeling issue. They have advised us that our school has not given proper instruction about the importance of our agricultural industries and how they support our country." He leans forward. "The *sustainable palm oil* industry in particular supports many farmers and provides prosperity to our economy in Indonesia. We are proud of this growth in our country."

"It's my country too," I say in Bahasa. Mom squeezes my hand tightly. Very tightly.

"We don't wish our students to become confused about this issue. Sustainable palm oil is supported by the government. It is true perhaps that *unregulated* palm oil plantations have caused damage in the past, but our leaders are doing everything in their power to ensure a safe and sustainable industry." He clears his throat. "The labeling issue is another misunderstanding. It is simply that the government wishes to support local products instead of foreign products. That's why the items in question were pulled from the supermarket shelves."

Mom is still squeezing my hand. It is only this that prevents me from blurting out that what he is saying is untrue. Untrue and unfair. Instead, we both remain silent.

"It is wonderful, of course, that Malia has shown an active interest in the environment," Mr. Ahmad goes on. "We have environmental clubs at the school that will welcome her participation. There are many organizations in Indonesia that are concerned with the welfare of threatened species and rehabilitation."

"How do you wish to proceed?" Mom asks, finally able to get a word in.

"Oh, very simply," he says, smiling now. "We have drafted a letter of apology to the government agency to which Malia directed her petition." He pulls a single piece of paper from his desk drawer and slides it toward Mom. He still hasn't acknowledged that I'm even in the room. "We just need Malia to sign the letter, and she can come back to school as usual. Actually, Malia has provided us with a valuable teaching opportunity." He finally turns to me. "You have given us the chance to see a hole in our curriculum, one that we can now repair."

I am sick to my stomach. My petition will result in students being taught something that is not completely true. They will be taught palm-oil propaganda, just like Hadi warned.

Mom is reading the apology statement quietly. After a few moments she looks up. "Malia and I will take this home and discuss the consequences of signing it," she says, gathering her handbag. "Thank you for your time."

The principal's smile fades. "I see, of course. Take your time, of course." His demeanor is suddenly stiff. "I must tell you that Malia cannot return unless this apology is signed." He leans back in his chair. "And I know that Mrs. Harwono is anxious to get back to work also."

"Surely it is up to Mrs. Harwono if she wishes to sign her apology letter, not Malia," Mom says, already standing.

"Oh, yes, Mrs. Harwono has already done so," he says. "But it will not have meaning unless both teacher *and* student apologize. Our direction from the local agricultural agency has been very clear. Without Malia's signature and admission of wrongdoing, it will be difficult for the school to support Mrs. Harwono's return to the classroom. Right now, it is seen that Mrs. Harwono is responsible for your daughter's misinformation."

"We both know that is untrue. We both know Mrs. Harwono is an excellent teacher and had nothing to do with the petition or the subject matter," Mom says to the principal, who is now also standing. "This was a student-directed assignment," Mom goes on. "Mrs. Harwono had no prior knowledge at all."

"Exactly. Mrs. Harwono is indeed a wonderful teacher, if perhaps a little too indulgent with her students. The assignment subjects should have been vetted by her first," he says. "In this matter, I'm afraid my hands are tied. We are a private school and therefore at the mercy of government-issued licensing."

Mom and I look at each other.

"The apology is just a formality, you understand," Mr. Ahmad goes on, his voice softening. "Just so we can get Malia and Mrs. Harwono back in the classroom where they belong." He brings out another paper from his drawer. "Your friend Putu understood this immediately. She and her family were very accommodating of our request earlier today."

He hands the paper to me and I see Putu's curvy signature across the bottom of the page.

"All that is left is your signature, Malia," he says. "If you don't sign, it will put your school, your friend, and your teacher all in, how do you say it in English? A sticky situation."

Ari

Melonie and Samir, now recovered from strep throat, have stepped up to coach the tournament team along with Yosef. They are like chess angels and do not seem the slightest bit upset not to be in the tournament themselves.

"Should I offer my position to one of them?" I ask Faisel. "It seems the right thing to do. I am just a beginner."

"Not possible," he answers. "It is against the rules to change tournament players after the qualifying rounds. Unless a player is ill. Anyway, you may be a beginner, but you are on a winning streak." He says this after I beat him again in a practice game. We are at the Warung Malang, where Uncle has offered the team a place to practice after the lunch rush. Yosef, Melonie, and Samir are soon to arrive with the two other members of the tournament team. Elvis Presley is bobbing up and down on his perch singing "You Ain't Nothin' But A Hound Dog," and Ginger Juice is lying on her back with her arm over her eyes, gripping the bars of her cage with her feet.

"I watched a documentary about orangutans once," Faisel says, glancing at her cage between moves. "They are very intelligent. The documentary showed how they could work out intricate games and puzzles. There was a term for it...." Faisel stops and thinks for a few seconds. "Enrichment activities," he says, remembering. "That's what the zookeepers called the games. The activities are designed to keep the apes' minds active. I even saw one of them painting."

"Really?" I ask, my interest piqued.

"Maybe she can play chess with you." Faisel chuckles as he sets up the board for another game.

"She'd probably win," I say, making a note to myself to search out some of these enrichment activities for her. Perhaps she could enjoy them in the larger enclosure I still want for her.

When the others arrive, Uncle Kus and Nang bring a tray of sweet tea out for us.

"Something for the chess champions to wet their whistles!" says Uncle. "Please, please, sit, drink, relax." He motions to the others as they attempt to stand and help with the tray. "I am happy for you to be here." He hands out the glasses before resting his hand on my shoulder. "I am very proud of my nephew. You are all welcome to practice here anytime."

I look at Uncle beaming at me and again marvel at his newfound lightness toward me. I resolve to think there are things in life that are better not to question and allow myself to enjoy his praise.

Yosef and Melonie stand by Elvis Presley's cage and applaud his musical performance, while Faisel and another team member try to coax Ginger Juice with a rambutan fruit. She does not rouse herself from her back, but she does take the small fruit between her toes. She suspends it above her head for a few moments, before dropping it where it rolls down her large belly. She repeats this a few times, much to the delight of her audience.

After the tea, I am paired up with Melonie. She smiles widely as she makes her opening move. Her bright eyes remind me of Suni. Even the way she wears her hijab is similar in style. It makes me realize how much I miss my cousin. Her quick laugh and witty chatter. As I watch Melonie and Samir talk quietly with each other, I am sure that if Suni were here, they would all become fast friends.

"Are you disappointed not to be in the tournament?" I ask Melonie.

"Not too much," she says. "Samir and I are training for an international tournament to be held in Yogyakarta later this year, so we have that to focus on. Besides, it's nice to coach for a change and help others."

"International tournament?" I ask. "There is such a thing? Who do you play against?"

"It is a tournament sponsored by the International Hotel

chain where the tournament will take place. Most of the players are from other countries in Southeast Asia, but sometimes from Europe too. It depends who qualifies."

"I didn't realize there were such events," I say.

"Oh, there are hundreds of tournaments all over the world, but one thing you must always remember," she says, keeping her finger on a chess piece and looking up at me. "Whether it is a school tournament or an international tournament, never let your opponent distract you with conversation." She slides her queen into checkmate position. "Never take your eyes from the board. Friendly banter can be fatal."

I smile. I don't mind the quick loss because she has just enlightened me with two glorious words: *international tournaments.*

"Is there prize money at these tournaments?" I ask her.

"Of course," she says, "but there are also entrance fees. And travel costs. Some highly ranked players have sponsors to help with their expenses."

"Do you have a sponsor?" I ask.

"No. Melonie and I are supported by our local mosque. They are very encouraging of our achievements. Our mothers and other women from our prayer community have even made us uniforms. They are a formidable cheering squad." She laughs. "And if we win any money, we donate it to the mosque for community programs."

"You don't keep any of the money?"

"No, but we get to stay in a hotel and eat at the restaurants and visit different cities. It's a lot of fun. We've been to Jakarta,

Kalimantan, and Bandung so far. And we get to raise money for the mosque. It's a blessing."

I shake my head at the easygoing goodwill of these girls, and I'm again reminded of Suni's sweet nature. I remember with shame having been glad to hear they were both sick with strep throat. I add this to my ever-increasing baggage of guilty feelings.

It could be the rush of a beginner on a winning streak, but the idea of playing chess beyond school tournaments is electrifying.

Suni was right in her letter. The universe is an enormous and wondrous place.

Malia

I stare at the apology letter, willing the words to rearrange themselves so I can bring myself to sign it. Mom was quiet on the drive back home.

"Malia, I'm not going to tell you what to do," she said once we'd pulled into our drive. "Signing or not signing the letter has consequences. Consequences that have come about because of your purposeful actions." She shook her head slowly, and I could tell she wished she could talk to Papa about what I have done. "You have all the information you need to reflect on the impact this has caused." She rested her hand on mine. "Once you've had some time to think it over, let's talk more." She found my gaze. "OK?"

"OK," I said.

Now I'm lying on my bed staring at the ceiling, turning everything over in my mind.

I want to sign the letter for Mrs. Harwono, but if I do, I am going against the truth. I am copping out on my activism.

If I don't sign the letter, I could be expelled and Mrs. Harwono could get fired.

If I am expelled, and don't have a school to attend, my fight to stay in Indonesia goes down the tubes.

And could I really carry Mrs. Harwono's firing on my conscience?

Then there's Putu. It stings that she was so quick to sign the letter. She didn't even text or call me to tell me what had happened in her meeting with Mr. Ahmad. I decide to call her. I dial her number, but it goes straight to voice mail. I don't leave a message, but text her instead.

Call me.

Then I throw my phone to the end of my bed and continue staring at the ceiling. I think of what started all of this in the first place: my wanting to save the orangutans, the petition against anti-palm oil labels, protesting about deforestation, and the orangutans' disappearing habitat. *What would Greta Thunberg do?* I wonder. I bet she wouldn't back down, no matter what. How can any real change occur if activists aren't willing to make tough choices? All of it swims around in my head. I hear the *ting* to alert me that I have a text. I sit up and grab my phone. It's Putu.

I'm not allowed to call you.

Seriously?

Yes. My parents are upset. They think you are a bad influence.

I'm sorry. I know about the apology letter. The principal showed it to me.

Did you sign it too?

Not yet.

Why?? You could get expelled!!

Because.... I stop texting, wishing I could just talk with her. *Can't you please just call me? I need to talk to you. Can you go out and call me?*

I don't hear anything again from Putu until an hour later. I'm still lying on my bed, but must have fallen asleep. The ringing of my phone wakes me up.

"It's me," she says. "I'm at the mall. I said I was meeting Susi."

"Are you seriously not allowed to be my friend anymore? Because of this?"

"I'm sure they will get over it," she says. "They are just really angry right now. Angry that we had to come back early from the cremation and angry that I was called into the principal's office. The school costs them a lot of money, and they see this as me disrespecting them."

"I'm sorry. I know I keep telling you I'm sorry, but I am. Truly."

"I know. Don't worry. Once you've signed the stupid letter, it will all go away."

I'm silent for a few moments.

"Don't tell me you're not going to sign it. Malia! Don't be

so stubborn. Mr. Ahmad said it will cause a lot of trouble if you don't sign it. What about Mrs. Harwono?"

"I know. It's just...it's..." I can't get the words out.

"It's what?" I can hear her exasperation.

"It's *wrong!*" I finally blurt.

"For who?" she says. "The orangutans? It's not going to make any difference to the orangutans if you sign the letter. It's just a dumb piece of paper."

"But if every activist who is trying to help the orangutans feels like that, nothing will ever change. If I sign the apology saying I was wrong, I have to lie. I have to say I support palm-oil! I can't do that." As I speak to Putu, I realize this is true. I can't sign the letter.

"I suppose it doesn't matter to you," Putu says, her voice cold now. "You can fly away to Canada and leave this mess behind you. What about Mrs. Harwono. What is she meant to do? This is so typical of you, Malia. So selfish. Can't you think of someone other than yourself for a change?"

"I'm not flying away anywhere," I say. "I'm staying here. I keep telling you that."

"Well, maybe you should go," she says. "Maybe that's better for everyone."

Her words shock us both into silence. Seconds tick by and fall into an icy void.

"I have to go now," she finally says and hangs up.

I didn't think it was possible to end the day feeling worse than I did when it started, but just like the first line of my presentation, *Impossible things happen all the time.*

Ari

On the way home from school, I stop at a roadside stall that sells art supplies.

"Can I have a children's paint set, please?" I ask. "Just a small one. And some paper."

The shopkeeper wraps the plastic paint tray in brown paper and rolls a few white sheets into a tube.

"You have to add water to the paintbrush," she says. "And rinse the brush in water each time you change colors, so they don't get mucky."

"Oh, of course," I say. "I'll need a paintbrush too, please."

"There's one included in the set," she says. "Just a small

one," she adds. She opens another box and shows me the thin brush inside. I can't imagine Ginger Juice holding something so small in her huge hand.

"I'm going to need a bigger one," I say, pointing to a larger, thicker brush displayed on the back wall of the stall.

The woman plucks it from the display, tapes it to the roll of paper, and tells me what I owe her. I dig into my pocket for the money. It is my week's budget for coffee and pastries at *Warung Kopi*.

I rush home, excited to bring the supplies back to Ginger Juice. I find her lying on her back, holding one foot aloft as she grooms the orange fur between each toe. I drag a table to her cage and unwrap the paints and paper.

"I have a game for us to play," I tell her. "We are going to paint!" I run off to the kitchen for a cup of water and scurry back again to see she is still focused on her foot grooming. "The experts call this an enrichment activity," I tell her. "Stimulation for your brain."

Ginger Juice is not roused by my chatter, but when I dip the wet paintbrush into the paint and draw strokes on the paper, see turns her head, her eyes following my every movement. She watches the activity intently. I continue making lines, circles, and dots from each color, until my paper is full. I hold my artwork up proudly.

"You see? It's called painting. Here," I say, sliding the paint tray and water cup through the bars of her cage. "Your turn." I unwrap a sheet of paper and lay it in the cage next to the paints and then hold up the larger paintbrush so she can see. "This is your brush. I bought it for you. Are you ready to try?"

Ginger Juice sits up finally and nudges at the paper with one foot, then she grips it in her toes and lies down again. She sniffs at the paper, now held high above her head.

"No, it's not food," I say. "It's a game." I waggle the paintbrush, still in my hand, for her to see. "It's for painting, like I was doing before." I hold up my page. "See?"

Ginger Juice places the paper over her face for a while, then holds it in her hands and begins to tear it into smaller and smaller pieces. This activity, at least, appears to interest her for a brief time, anyway. Once the pieces are too small, she rolls onto her side, facing away from me. Her shifting around knocks over the cup, spilling the water over the paint set. The paint-stained water is now seeping into the newspaper that I put down in her cage this morning.

"I guess we will need further art lessons," I tell her, more than a little disappointed. I had imagined she would be immediately engaged with the activity. At least I saved the paintbrush from ruin. "We will try again tomorrow," I say, gathering up the paint tray and cup from her cage. Ginger Juice has lost all interest and is lying on her back again, grooming her foot. Perhaps she is not like the orangutans that Faisel saw on television after all.

I turn to see that Uncle has been watching from the restaurant and is now chuckling. "You are a funny lad," he says. "Painting for an ape? This is not kindergarten, my boy. She's just a dumb creature. She doesn't want to play silly games." He laughs. "What's next? Teaching her to play chess?" He grins at me in a good-natured way and pats my shoulder as I pass him to drop the mess in the garbage. "Leave her be. She just wants peace and quiet. Trust me, I know what is best for her."

My plan to show Uncle that Ginger Juice deserves a larger enclosure and more stimulation is torn to shreds, just like the painting I throw into the garbage can.

Ginger Juice

Is night.

Humans creep across grass in darkness and stand around cage. They hold things in hands to drink from, swaying and laughing. Scent smells bad. Rotten fruit smell. Bad smell mix with smoke from small burning sticks humans hold in fingers.

I not know what they want.

Elvis Presley shrieks warning call under hood. Humans speak words I not understand. They *tap, tap, tap* the drinking things on bars of cage. Rotten fruit smell is coming from inside the drinking things and now, I smell of it too. Humans splash the stinking water over me.

I try to move away but cannot do. Arms stiff, legs weak. More rotting water splash in face.

Humans laughing. I confused. Why they make me smell rotten? Why is funny?

I hide face in corner of cage. I want them disappear.

Human grabs hand. I let him. Maybe it will be like when Slow Loris Boy holds hand. But no. No warmth. No gentle. Feel sting. Sting gets bigger. Hurting, burning! Like forest burning.

I cry, pull my hand and lick, lick finger to feel better. Elvis Presley shrieks and shrieks. I want humans go away. Why they hurt me? Try to hide. Nowhere to hide.

I call haze to come. I want fear feelings to stop burrowing in head.

Ari

In the early morning when I go to greet Ginger Juice and clean out her cage, I notice a few beer bottles have been thrown on the grass surrounding her enclosure. On further inspection I see cigarette butts have been stamped out all around the cage. I peer through the bars. "Good morning, Ginger Juice," I say. She doesn't respond to my voice. She is lying, faceup, with her arms crossed over her eyes. I look more closely and see that the hair on her arms and chest is matted with liquid. I look at the beer bottles around the cage. *Could it be beer? What has happened? Who has done this?* My mind races with the horrible images of harm that might have befallen her.

Michelle Kadarusman

"Ginger Juice, what happened?" I ask her stupidly. "Did someone hurt you?"

She still does not meet my gaze. Instead, she lifts her arms to look above my head at the morning sky. Then her chin slumps heavily on her chest, eyes cast downward. Her arms lie listlessly against her sides. I reach through the bars and touch her hand. She flinches, but before she pulls away, I see a round, raised mark on the pad of her finger. It is a small circular burn, the size of a cigarette tip. Bile rises up in my throat as I realize what has happened. Someone has burned her with their cigarette. They have poured beer over her and they have burned her. The cruelty doubles me over and I vomit on the grass. Tears of sorrow and anger run down my cheeks as I grip the bars of the cage. "I will get you out of here," I tell her. "I promise."

I march to the restaurant and find Uncle and Nang squeezing jeruk for the day's fresh ginger juice.

"Come and see!" I am yelling. "Come and see what has happened!"

"What? What is it? What's wrong?" Uncle jumps up from his stool. "Calm yourself, boy. Tell me what has happened."

"Come and see for yourself," I say, running back to Ginger Juice's cage. Uncle follows behind and soon comes upon the beer bottles on the grass. "What a mess," he says kicking at an empty bottle with his sandaled foot. "Those scoundrel kids."

"The little neighborhood kids? No. There's beer and cigarettes. Do you know who did this?" I ask.

"Older kids...young people, maybe a little older than you. I thought I heard them last night. It was late."

120

"Look," I say, pointing to Ginger Juice. "Look what they did to her!"

Uncle shakes his head, not really looking at Ginger Juice, but at the cigarette butts and bottles instead. "We'll have to get a security light. One of those lights that turn on with movement. It will scare off any kids if they try and come in again."

"Is that all you can say?" I splutter. "Look at her!"

"What do you mean?" he asks. "I see her right there."

"But *look* at her," I implore him. "They poured beer on her. She's been burned. She's been tormented." My hands are holding both sides of my head so it doesn't explode. "Don't you care?"

"Of course, I care. I will get a motion light, just as I said. It won't happen again." He glances at Ginger Juice briefly. "Get the hose and clean her off." Uncle walks back to the kitchen.

"You can't keep her in this cage any longer!" I shout at his back. "It is wrong. It's cruel!" I wait for him to turn around before I continue. "We need to find a better place for her. Somewhere she can live like an ape, not an—*attraction!* Do you even know that it's illegal to keep her in captivity?"

Uncle's calm demeanor breaks, and he stalks toward me, his finger is pointed between my eyes. "How dare you say these things? She belongs to *me!*" He thumps his chest. "She is not your concern!" he shouts. "She is not going anywhere. What would the restaurant patrons think if they came and she was gone? We would lose customers!" His eyes narrow. "Be careful nephew, she is needed here far more than you are. Now clean up this mess!" I watch as he stomps back to the kitchen, my chest pounding, my ears hot. I look to Ginger

Juice again and see she has covered her ears. Our shouting has further upset her.

"I'm sorry, I'm sorry," I say to her softly. "It's OK, don't worry. It's OK." I keep speaking platitudes, as much for my nerves as hers, but she doesn't respond. Her head rocks gently side to side, she is still covering her ears.

I know what Uncle is saying. I can read between the lines. He is saying that if I cause any trouble, if I threaten again to free Ginger Juice, he will send me back to the village. He will send me back, and there will be no more school, no more chess, no more of anything except planting rice.

Malia

Mom had a call from the university this morning, some kind of mishap with her examination scores, so she's rushing out the door.

"You may as well go to tea with your grandmother as usual," she says. "Your oma doesn't know anything about what's happened at your school. Not from me, anyway. But knowing her, she'll find out. You should tell her." She stops and looks at me. "How did you do, thinking it over last night? Wait. Don't answer now," she says. "We'll talk about this properly when I get home."

"OK," I say. "See you later."

Michelle Kadarusman

Ever since I was eight years old, I have met Oma at the Shangri-La Hotel for afternoon tea. Oma adopted the English tradition when she was studying in London, decades ago. Studying abroad is common for wealthy Indonesians like Oma, and according to her, the Shangri-La is the only place that does afternoon tea properly. The Shangri-La is a five-star hotel that is popular with tourists and affluent locals. My grandmother owns a chain of *apotek*. She started with one pharmacy and within a dozen years she had multiple drugstores dotted all across Surabaya and East Java. As a young woman, she had studied pharmaceutical sciences, but after returning to Indonesia, it soon became clear that her real passion was business.

I arrive at the hotel before her, and the maître d' recognizes me. "Good afternoon, Miss," he says in English. "*Selamat sore*," I reply in Bahasa. He escorts me to Oma's usual table in the luxurious lobby restaurant overlooking lush gardens around a glistening swimming pool. I sit down to wait, folding my hands in my lap, and plan out what I am going to say to my grandmother. She is my last hope of staying in Indonesia. I need her help.

I watch as a group of Western tourists lines up at the reception desk. They are sweaty and fanning themselves with magazines, visibly relieved to have escaped the blistering heat outside. Two small children break free from their parents and run across the lobby toward the large glass windows. They bang their small hands on the glass, pointing and squealing joyfully to see the swimming pool.

My oma arrives and I watch her glide through the marble lobby, nodding and waving demurely to her many acquaintances who are also dining in the lobby restaurant. For my grandmother and her peers, it is important that the prestige of patronizing the hotel is seen and acknowledged. It would hardly be worth the hefty price tag otherwise, billed in US dollars.

When she reaches the table, Oma bends to graze her soft cheek against mine, once on each side. Her fingers move lightly as she unwraps an expensive silk scarf from her neck. It matches the headscarf she is wearing that remains perfectly in place. Under the headscarf her hair is dyed jet black. One of the two waiters who have floated silently behind her offers to take her coat. She slides her arms from the tailored business jacket, not required in the heat, but worn for fashion. The other waiter expertly folds it and places it neatly on the chair next to her as she is seated. The waiters now hover nervously at each arm, awaiting instruction. Once Oma has given her usual order, they scurry away to fulfill it, their steps muffled by the plush carpets.

"Hello, darling," she says. "You look tired. So young and already dark circles around your eyes. Aren't you sleeping well?"

"Not really," I admit. "I'm stressed."

Oma takes a sip of ice water, raising a shaped eyebrow. "Oh, really? About what?"

"I don't want to move to Toronto," I tell her. "I want to live with you. I want to stay here in Surabaya."

"I see," she says. We study each other. "Your mother would never agree," she says. "And neither would I." She gives me a small smile. "Although I would love to say yes, it would not be the right thing to do. You belong with your mother. But you will spend your school vacations with me. I will visit you in Toronto often. And one day, when you are older, you can come and live with me, if you choose. But not now. Now is your time to be with your mother."

"But why? You don't even like Mom."

"That is not so. Your mother and I do not agree on many things. We have different views, different customs, but I have always respected her. She is true to her heart, true to her beliefs. And she loves you very much."

"But I want to stay here," I say, making an effort to keep the whine from my voice. "I am Indonesian. I don't know who I will be in Canada."

"Dear girl. You are not defined by where you live or where your parents were born or where you were born. You are defined by what is in your heart, by your actions, your words.

"Look at me," she continues. "My father was born in Jakarta, my mother was born in Singapore. I am a business-woman. I am a Muslim woman, I am Indonesian, I am Javanese, I was educated in Europe. I live in Surabaya, but once upon a time I lived abroad." She gives me a challenging look. "Who am I? Try to give me one label."

"You are my Oma."

She smiles. "Yes. To you, I am your grandmother because that is what is in my heart for you, and my actions and words tell you this is true. But to others, my employees for example, I am someone else. Do you follow? You are what is in your heart, you impact others by your actions and your words. Remember this, my love. Indonesian. Canadian. Girl. Woman. Mother.

Daughter. Grandmother. If you limit yourself to labels you are only putting yourself in a cage."

"But it's Indonesia that is in my heart," I murmur. It's an effort to fend off the avalanche of disappointment that threatens to crush me. *Who gets rejected by their own grandmother?*

"Sometimes you need to let other places into your heart too. Trust me, there will be space enough in your heart for many places, many people. You will have to take my word on it."

A tiered cake platter arrives with an assortment of sandwiches, cakes, cookies, and scones. The waiters also carry a large teapot, from which they pour tea. The steam rises from the liquid in the porcelain teacups and evaporates in the frigid air conditioning.

"Enough of that talk now," she says. "Drink your tea." Oma swivels the platter, positioning the macaron cookies in front of my plate. "Here, I know these are your favorite."

I sip my tea obediently and take a mouthful of cookie, struggling to swallow it. I keep chewing, trying to ignore the tightening across my ribs and the tears that creep into the corners of my eyes. I bite my lip to keep the waterworks at bay. Oma is not someone who will tolerate further argument. I know she expects me to be strong, like her.

"And what about this other business," she asks in between small sips of tea. "What have you been up to at your school, *hmm*?"

"You heard about it?"

"Of course I heard about it. I pay your school tuition, remember?"

"I'm sorting it out," I say. "I'm fixing it." I don't want to ask her advice because I know what she will say and I don't want to hear it. My grandmother is what you would call *establishment*. She has done well in business because she does not ruffle feathers. And she smooths things over where they need to be smoothed. Saving orangutans is not on her to-do list. Making money is her priority. Papa, her only son, was very different.

"Be sure you do," she says pointedly.

I had caught a taxi to the Shangri-La, so after our tea Oma says she will have her driver drop me home. She will stay on at the lobby restaurant and meet with her friends. Oma hands me the box of leftover sweets and does not let go of my hand.

"Don't think that I will not miss you when you go, Granddaughter," she says, squeezing my hand. "I will miss you more than words can express, especially..." She stops herself from speaking the words, but they hang in the air anyway. Neither of us wants to drag up our hard-trodden grief for Papa. "This is your time to be brave and strong," she says instead. "And one thing I have always known about you is that you *are* strong, just like me. Now it's time for your courage to shine." She is still seated, so I bend down to kiss both her cheeks. She whispers so softly into my ear that I wonder if she has spoken at all. "Staying will not bring him back," she says.

The uniformed bellman nods to me as Oma's black Mercedes pulls into the wide circular drive of the hotel. Oma's driver, Gamin, jumps out to open the door for me. He has worked for Oma for as long as I can remember. "Hello, Miss Malia," he says politely.

BERANI

I sit in the backseat of Oma's Mercedes, and Gamin waits for a chance to merge into the heavy traffic. A girl my age with a toddler, wrapped in a sarong across her chest, taps lightly on the window to get our attention. The small child she carries is likely a younger sibling. They are both covered in a layer of grime from the car fumes and dust along the busy road. The girl's hand is outstretched in a silent plea for coins.

"Do you have any small money?" I ask Gamin.

"Yes, Miss," he says, and reaches into the glove compartment. He rolls down his window and drops a few coins into the girl's palm. She nods but does not smile. The toddler, all the while, seems to stare, wide-eyed, directly at me. But I know that is impossible because the glass is tinted. I lower my window. "Here," I say to the girl, giving her the box of leftover sweets. "I hope you like these." She takes them but still does not smile. *Why should she?* I think. *Pastries and cookies will do nothing to solve her problems.* Beggars on the streets of Surabaya are common. The unrelenting poverty is everywhere.

I know that girl could just as easily be me. It could be me standing outside an expensive hotel wondering why I am hungry, while other people arrive in luxury cars and are ushered inside to eat cake. Cake they don't even bother to finish.

I hear Papa's words, the words he would always say when I asked why others were poor and we were not. *The poor are poor through no fault of their own. The rich are rich not because we are superior. You must always show kindness. You must always be grateful. You must never take your blessings for granted.* I'd heard those words so many times, but I had never really thought deeply about their meaning. Now, seeing the look of despair on the street girl holding my discarded box of treats, it illuminates the depth of his sentiments.

Shame wells inside me, and the tears come. I had fought them back throughout my visit with Oma, but now they come flooding out in heavy sobs. *I'm sorry Papa. I'm sorry.* I continue to sob. Gamin glances at me in his rearview mirror before quickly looking away again. He doesn't want to embarrass me. The street girl's face is replaced with Mom's, Putu's, Bibi's, Mrs. Harwono's. The selfishness of my actions toward all of them takes my breath away.

All Papa had asked, even in his last words to me, was to treat people with kindness, and I have failed, failed, failed miserably.

Ari

I wake up, my body stiff from sleeping on the ground. I slept next to Ginger Juice's cage last night, not wanting to leave her, in case whoever had harmed her the night before returned.

I rub my neck and stretch my legs. Someone, likely Nang, put a sarong over me in the night. I fold the batik cloth now and sit on top of it. The earth is cool and damp. A rooster crows nearby, signaling the early dawn. The dewy freshness of the morning air will soon give way to a heavy blanket of heat.

I look at Ginger Juice in the hazy, blue morning light. She is lying on her stomach, her face cradled in her arms, her legs curled into her body. She lies very still but she is not asleep. She watches me with sad eyes. I see her lips move, and she is gesturing to me with her long index finger. It looks like she is trying to tell me something, but how would I ever know what it is? *Are there people in the world who can communicate with orangutans? Are there really people who can help Ginger Juice have a better life?*

The striking girl with the caramel eyes flashes into memory. The one I saw at the private school. The one who handed me the paper. "Wait!" I tell Ginger Juice and dash to my room. I find my satchel and search the bottom of it for the petition the girl gave me weeks ago. My hand finds a scrunched-up ball of paper and I run back to Ginger Juice's cage with it. I sit again on the sarong and unfold the tattered sheet. I find my reading glasses lying on the grass where I left them last night. I reread the information about what to do if you know of a captive orangutan.

KEEPING ORANGUTANS AS PETS IS AGAINST THE LAW. IF YOU KNOW OF ONE BEING HELD IN CAPTIVITY YOU SHOULD CALL THE AUTHORITIES. CAPTIVE ORANGUTANS CAN BE RESCUED AND SENT TO REHABILITATION CENTERS WHERE THEY CAN LIVE IN CONDITIONS MORE LIKE THEIR NATURAL ENVIRONMENT. SOMETIMES THEY CAN BE RETURNED TO THE WILD. WITH SO FEW ORANGUTANS LEFT IN THE WILD, EVERY CAPTIVE ORANGUTAN IS IMPORTANT. DON'T REMAIN SILENT IF YOU CAN HELP A CAPTIVE ORANGUTAN.

Authorities? What authorities? Most of Uncle's friends, his domino pals, are army personnel. They *are* the authority around here. There is no telephone number, no Web site address on the petition, except for a government agency to send the petition to. But wait. There is another e-mail address, the girl's own. Her name is Malia Kusarto, and I have her e-mail address.

"I think I've found someone who can help us," I tell Ginger Juice. "We are going to get you out of here."

But Ginger Juice has closed her eyes now. Whether she is asleep, or just tired of what she sees, I don't know. I sit with her until the sun fully rises and my stomach growls for food. I didn't eat anything all of yesterday. I couldn't keep anything down, but this morning my appetite has returned. I go to the kitchen, still too early even for Uncle and Nang, and scoop a ladle of cold rice into a bowl and take a salted duck egg from the pantry. I take my plate back to Ginger Juice's cage, but she has not opened her eyes again. I eat my food, chewing, thinking, chewing. Things are much clearer now. I know what I must do. Building a larger encloser is not enough. Engaging Ginger Juice with activities is not enough. She is not lazy. She doesn't move because her arms and legs are weak from years of captivity. Deep down, I have always known this. Deep down, I have known that keeping her locked in a cage is cruel. *It is cruel and she is suffering.* I cannot fool myself about this any longer.

I keep watching her face and the rise and fall of her large chest. She is slipping away from this world, I can feel it in my bones. I hope I am not too late to save her.

Malia

Mom is still at the university when I get home from the
Shangri-La. I'm glad. This gives me time to do what I need
to do. I get my laptop and start writing. It doesn't take me
long—I know exactly what I want to say. I hit Print at the
same moment I hear Mom's car pull into our driveway.

I still feel emotional and weepy after crying in Oma's car, so
when I see Mom walk through the front door, I run to her and
throw my arms around her. I hold on tight, burying my face in
her shoulder.

"Hey, hey," she says, stroking my hair. "What's going on?"

"I'm not going to sign their apology letter," I say, pulling away finally. "I have written my own statement instead."

"Ah, I see," she says, wiping a stray tear from my cheek. "Let's go and sit down so I can read it."

We walk to the living room, Mom still with her arm around my shoulder. We sit on the couch, and Mom takes the paper I hand to her.

"Before you read this, there is something else I need to tell you," I say.

I hold my arm up next to hers, and we look at the different skin tones, my mocha and her vanilla. "Maybe I'm ready to try some maple syrup with my mocha ice cream," I say.

Mom laughs and kisses the top of my head. "There is no one else like you, Malia."

I rest my head on her shoulder as she reads my letter.

LETTER OF APOLOGY FROM MALIA KUSARTO

To Whom It May Concern,

Recently I gave a presentation at my school about deforestation and the destruction of the habitats of orangutans to make room for palm oil plantations in Indonesia. I made a petition for my fellow students to sign, protesting the removal of products labeled palm-free from our supermarkets.

My teacher, Mrs. Harwono, did not know about the subject I planned to present. I disobeyed my mother, who asked me to inform my teacher about my presentation. Once I had completed my presentation and circulated the petition, Mrs. Harwono collected the papers from the students and told me I was not allowed to circulate them until she got permission from our school principal. I disobeyed her instructions and sent the petition online through my class Web page. I also lied to my best friend, who was not aware I was purposefully disobeying both my mother and my teacher.

For this, I am deeply sorry. I apologize to my mother, my teacher, my school, and my best friend.

If my actions have caused others to suffer, I am truly sorry and want to take responsibility for this. Mrs. Harwono is a wonderful teacher, and it is my hope that my actions do not result in her being punished.

What I cannot apologize for is speaking about environmental awareness and the impact of palm oil agriculture on orangutans. This is an issue that I intend to continue to learn more about. I also intend to continue my activism.

Yours truly,
Malia Kuswarto

Mom puts down the paper. "You are one tough cookie," she says. "But I admire your principles. And I am glad to see you are taking responsibility for the harm you have caused others." She pauses. "I hate saying things like this, but I hope you've learned your lesson." She nods. "This takes guts, Malia."

"Not really," I say. "It's easy for me to stand by my principles because I am privileged. I have you and Oma and, for now, I don't have to worry about making a living. Not like Mrs. Harwono." I stare at the letter. "Do you think this will help her?"

"Hadi has spoken with her. He will speak with the principal if the school does not reinstate her. Hadi and Mr. Ahmad have mutual friends in local government, but he will try to make sure it doesn't get that far. According to Hadi, what the principal told us is all bluff." She sighs. "Let's hope so, anyway."

"I hope so," I say. "I *really* hope so."

"Why don't you send this to Mrs. Horwono before you send it to the principal?" Mom suggests. "Give her a chance to respond this time."

"Good idea," I say. "I have her e-mail address. I'll send it to Putu as well."

I get my laptop from my room and go into my e-mail account. I have been avoiding my inbox since my school suspension. Once I log on, I see that I've received over fifty e-mails. I scroll through names I recognize from school and others I don't recognize at all. I'll get to them later.

I find Mrs. Harwono's e-mail address and spend time

writing her a personal apology and then attach my statement. I hit send, hoping she will allow me to call her, so I can apologize in person. Then I write to Putu.

> I know you are mad at me. And I know I deserve it. I hope you can forgive me. You are the most fantastic best friend I could ever hope to have. I am sorry for causing all of this trouble for you and your family. And I'm sorry for all of the times I have been selfish. You definitely deserve a lot better. I hope you can give me another chance to be a better friend.

> Love, Malia

Before I close my computer, I scan the inbox again. I see by the e-mail titles that most are congratulating me, or commiserating with me, some have clapping emojis or crying-face emojis. But a few have red-faced, angry emojis. One e-mail catches my attention. It's titled *Captive Orangutan* and it's from someone named Ari Arjuna.

Ari

I want to keep my vigil by Ginger Juice's cage, but now I must leave her to attend school. After sending the e-mail to Malia Kusarto, I am anxious for her response. I want to know her advice for Ginger Juice's rescue.

After I sent the e-mail at the Internet Café, I did a brief online search for orangutan rescues, and a few different organizations popped up. It seems there are established sanctuaries in both Borneo and Sumatra. I didn't even know there are three different species of orangutans, depending on where they are from. All I know about Ginger Juice is that her mother was killed, and she was "saved" by Uncle's army pal. One thing is certain. If I go forward with having her rescued, Uncle will never speak to me again. My days of living under his roof will be over. Which means attending school will be over as well. Not only that, but Uncle could potentially face trouble from the authorities. It is illegal to keep an orangutan, but I also read no Indonesian has ever been charged with this crime. Still, it is a risk.

Am I willing to proceed knowing what could happen? I think of my parents and of Suni. *If I can't live at Uncle's place and I can't attend school, I will be squandering their hard-earned tuition fees.* The weight of what I intend to do settles on my shoulders like the yoke we put on our water buffalo that ploughs the rice fields.

I'm not sure why I do it, but I give Ginger Juice the sarong I have been sitting on. She immediately unfolds it and covers herself. She disappears underneath the cloth with only a single foot poking out from her sarong tent.

I reach through the bars and stroke her foot. She is motionless, as still as a statue. It is perhaps my imagination, but since the attack it is as though she is slipping farther and farther away. She sits here, but it is like her mind and her spirit are dissolving. *I cannot allow her life to wither away before my eyes. I must have her rescued and I will bear the consequences.*

As difficult as this decision is, I know it is right. I am finally ready to address the rat-gnawing feelings of guilt that I have been carrying for so long.

Malia

I see Mrs. Harwono's name come up on my phone, and my heart skips. I answer the call nervously.

"I'm sorry," I blurt into the phone before she has had a chance to say anything. "I'm so sorry. I never meant to cause you so much trouble. I didn't think sending the petition would get you..." I stop and think about what is really true. "No. I just didn't think," I admit. "I didn't think how it would affect you at all." I grip the phone tighter. "I'm so sorry."

"I will not pretend you haven't caused me anguish, Malia," she says. "This situation has been very stressful. I've had many sleepless nights over it. But I do appreciate your honest apology and I understand why you didn't sign the draft that the principal gave you."

I wait anxiously to hear whether Mrs. Harwono has been fired. I am holding my breath.

"You can rest easy," she says. "I will return to the classroom tomorrow."

Relief washes over me. "The principal made it sound like you would be fired if I didn't sign the statement."

"You have to understand. He is getting pressure from the local government," she says. "He wants to appease them."

"Is that why you signed the statement?" I ask.

"We all have to make our own judgments and decisions based on what is best for ourselves and our families."

"And will you teach the palm-oil propaganda now?" I ask.

"Teaching can take many forms. I can present a subject to students, and those like you will always seek out more information." She pauses. "Perhaps I will use this very example of a former student who dared to send a petition to the government." She says this with humor in her voice. But hearing her describe me as a "former student" stings. It brings to surface the reality of what I have done.

Mrs. Harwono is silent for a moment. "Indonesia needs young people like you, Malia, who love their country enough to stand up when they believe something is unjust."

"I do love my country," I say. "But I have to go with my Mom to Canada. I will come back."

BERANI

"I believe you will. My guess is that one day you will return, and your love of this land will be put to good use."

"I *will* be back," I tell her. "I promise you that."

Ari

I drop in at the Internet Café after school hoping for a reply from Malia Kusarto, but my inbox remains empty. My chess team is waiting for me to come to practice, but I stay at the café to do more research on orangutan rescue instead. Chess has become less important in comparison to my worry for Ginger Juice.

I revisit the Web sites of the rescue organizations in Borneo and Sumatra that I discovered earlier. There is a huge amount of information, and my head swims with it all. My stomach lurches when I read passages about the physical and mental deterioration that occurs when orangutans are held captive.

Images of apes so much like Ginger Juice stare out at me from the computer screen, seeming to implore me to help. One Web site challenges the reader to imagine how a human would react to living their entire life in a cage. The DNA of humans and orangutans is so close, it states, that the same level of mental suffering is highly likely.

My temples throb as I jot down telephone numbers of the organizations. I put the scrap of paper in my pocket and hurry home to Ginger Juice. Each time I leave her I fret about what I will find when I return. Visiting the Web sites and seeing the images of other orangutans only heightens my anguish for her.

Malia

I didn't get expelled! In the end it was all bluff, just a storm in a teacup, as Hadi said it would be. Mr. Ahmad had been doing what was in his power to appease the government agents, and they must have felt assured that no further disruption would be coming from his students. Or perhaps Oma had something to do with it.

Still, the whole experience has made me look at my behavior differently, and I've decided that to protect my friends and teachers, I will keep my schoolwork and activism separate from now on.

Mom and I have made a plan to finish our school terms

here before our move to Toronto in May. Mom thinks it will be a good idea for me to have a few months in Toronto before school starts in September. Acclimatization, she calls it. And we can spend the summer at the family lakeside cottage. It's scary to imagine living in a new country, but seeing the lightness in Mom's eyes as she anticipates being close to my grandparents and uncles again, I know it's the right thing.

When Mom got the news that I could start school again, I texted Putu. She had replied to my apology e-mail saying that she'd forgiven me, but her parents still needed time for things to settle down before they'd agree to let her see me again. She admitted that maybe she needed a little time too. Now that I was officially out of the school's bad books, I hoped enough time had passed.

Is my jail sentence over? Can we talk now?

Always so dramatic, you

So, we are friends again?

As if you would stand for anything else

You know me so well LOL

Yes, I do ☺

You better book your ticket to come and see me in Toronto

So you are really going? ☹

You were right. As usual. It's the best thing to do for my Mom

You are brave, I wish I was more like you

Please stay exactly as you are. We balance each other out, remember

LOL ♥

When you come to Canada, I'll take you tobogganing

Stop teasing me!

I love u

I love u more

I put my phone down and smile to myself. It feels like a missing chink in my heart has been returned to where it belongs.

I open my laptop. I know there are other messages I should reply to. As soon as I go into my inbox, I notice the e-mail from Ari Arjuna again. I've been so distracted with the petition and Mrs. Harwono that I'd forgotten about it.

I open it and read the message.

Ari writes that he lives in Malang and is also in seventh grade. He visited my school for a chess tournament, and I gave him a paper copy of my petition. He wants my help to rescue an orangutan that lives at his uncle's restaurant. Her name is Ginger Juice. Ari includes a telephone number where he can be reached. I pick up my phone and dial it.

Ari

Nang calls to me from the kitchen, she says I have a telephone call. I go in and take the receiver.

"Hello?"

A girl's voice. A confident voice. "Hi Ari, this is Malia Kuswarto. You e-mailed me."

"Malia. Hi," I say. "It's you." I am surprised. "I was expecting an e-mail, but this is better. Thanks for calling me."

"Sure," she says. "So, you have an orangutan? Really?"

"Yes...but it is not a good situation. She needs to be rescued." I swallow, wishing I could speak with Malia's confidence, but I can't. "You seem to know a lot about it...about

153

orangutans," I go on. "So, I thought maybe you could help us."

"Yes, for sure," she says. "I could give you the contact number for a rescue organization that does really good work here in East Java."

"I did some research of my own, but I'm not sure of the best place to call," I admit.

We compare notes on the various organizations and Malia suggests which one I should call.

"Can I ask you a favor, Ari?" she asks.

"Of course," I say.

"Could I be there for the rescue? I would be super interested to meet you and see Ginger Juice. I'm really interested in animal activism. I'd love to see a rescue firsthand."

"That would be great," I tell her. "To be honest, I'm really nervous. My uncle is going to be pretty angry at me when he finds out."

Malia chuckles. "I know what that feels like," she says. "I've gotten myself into trouble lately as well. I'd be happy to support what you're doing. You can count on me."

We speak for a few more minutes and my nervousness ebbs away. Malia has an assertive, yet calm way about her. Very reassuring. But when I try to give her directions to Malang, she cuts me off.

"I know where Malang is, Ari," she says in a testy tone. "I've lived in Surabaya my whole life." I smile to myself when I remember one of her schoolmates describing her as bossy.

We say good-bye, and I promise to get back in touch when I have a date for the rescue.

BERANI

Speaking with Malia buoys my courage to contact the orangutan organization. It is as though some of her bravery has rubbed off on me. Knowing she will be here when it happens fills me with comfort, which is odd, considering we don't know each other very well.

I find the telephone number of the organization we discussed and draw a circle around it. I will call them tomorrow when Uncle is at Friday prayers.

For days now, Ginger Juice has not come out from underneath the sarong. Her once constant grooming and inspection of her fur has ceased. She lies motionless under the cloth.

I am having difficulty concentrating on schoolwork and I have been letting down my chess team members. After so many missed practices, Yosef found me yesterday to say that I would lose my spot in the tournament if I kept skipping.

"Please let Samir or Melonie take my place," I told him. "I'm sorry."

"Are you unwell?" Yosef asked me. "That is the only way we can make a replacement."

"Unwell? Yes," I replied. "You can definitely say I am unwell."

I go now to Ginger Juice's cage and pace around her enclosure. My everyday life has been tipped upside down. Nothing feels normal anymore. I cannot rest until I get her out of this cage. I feel caged myself, caged in my own worry. I am beginning to understand that no living thing is meant to be contained. I also resolve to find a place to send Elvis Presley.

I do feel somewhat better though, knowing I now have a friend in Malia Kusarto.

Ginger Juice

I hide under thing Slow Loris Boy gives me. This thing hide me like giant taro leaf. It has scent of human, but helps me disappear.

Better here in dark where haze come and take me away. Under here, I don't see bars of cage. Under here do not see humans come hurt me.

Under here, maybe can disappear from cage. Slide between bars and roll, roll, roll on grass. Fill nose with scent of dirt and leaves.

Stay in darkness and let haze take me away.

In dark no matter my arms weak, my body slow. And fear

feelings, like termites burrowing into dead tree trunks, go away.

I tired. So tired, Ibu. So tired live in this place. I stay under here until eyes do not open again. Maybe I find you in darkness. Have nowhere else to look for you.

Ari

It is Friday. I tell Uncle I am not feeling well and will not join him at the mosque. He tells me to get some rest and leaves the restaurant. Nang is taking care of the few patrons who have stopped in for a late lunch. As soon as Uncle is gone, I go into the restaurant office and sit at his desk. This is where I usually do the bookkeeping. My heart hammers in my chest as I pick up the telephone receiver. I take the slip of paper with the phone number written on it and dial. Malia's fiery gaze flashes before my eyes and gives me a boost of courage.

"Hello? Hello? Is anyone there?" Someone is on the other

end of the line, and I have been just holding the receiver, saying nothing.

"Yes. Hello. My name is Ari Arjuna. I am calling you from Malang in East Java."

"How I can I help you, Ari?" It is a woman's voice. Very calm and friendly.

"I want to inform you of an orangutan who is being kept as a pet," I say. "No. Not a pet exactly. Not anymore. She is an attraction. She is kept in a cage." I take a breath. "She needs to be rescued." I pause. "I want her to have a better life."

From there it all happens breathtakingly fast. The woman tells me she will transfer my call to the person who handles orangutan rescues, and she does. This time a man comes on the line and speaks in a professional tone. He tells me he needs details so he can dispatch a rescue team.

My voice shakes as I give him our exact location. "My Uncle...he will not be in trouble, will he?"

"Not if he cooperates, no."

"What if he doesn't?" I ask.

The man is silent for a moment. "The veterinarian with the rescue team will explain to your uncle that it is against the law to keep an orangutan, and that he must cooperate. They will explain that to keep a wild animal as a pet is dangerous to both the animal and the humans it comes into contact with. It is important your uncle understands this, so he does not do it again. A police officer will be with the team to ensure everything goes smoothly."

The man goes on to ask many questions about Ginger Juice, her age, her appearance, her health, her eating habits.

"You are doing the right thing, Ari," he says. "The conditions she is living in are not acceptable. Orangutans are extremely intelligent apes. It is likely she is suffering from both mental and physical deterioration. She is not able to exercise, so her muscles will be wasting away and she is most likely overweight. This can lead to diabetes. We will make sure she gets the help she needs."

When I tell him the opening of the cage is too small for her to get out, he says they will sedate her and they will use a chainsaw to cut through the bars.

"Sadly, the rescue team has done this many times before," he says. "Many people do not know what to do once an orangutan is no longer a small, cuddly baby. Putting them in a cage seems to be a good solution at first until they outgrow the cage. Often this is when we are called." He pauses. "Wild animals are not pets."

"I know. I know it's wrong, what we have done," I tell him, tasting salt on my lips from the tears that are dripping down my cheeks. "But...I will miss her."

Agonizing days pass before I receive an e-mail from the orangutan organization. They have mobilized a rescue team in my area and have scheduled the date. They will arrive in the early evening, as I requested. I didn't want the rescue to occur when the restaurant is open. I can at least protect Uncle from the embarrassment of this happening in front of his patrons.

I have now put an event in motion that cannot be stopped. One that, depending on how he reacts, might land my uncle in jail.

Malia

Mom and I decide to take a weekend trip to Bali.

Our place to stay in Bali is a *losman* in the Ubud hills. My experience of the popular holiday island is not of surfers and sandy beaches, but of emerald-green rice terraces and banana pancakes.

My parents discovered the losman before I was born, and we've gone there so often that I think of it as my own holiday home. The guesthouse is a simple Balinese style villa with a covered pavilion overlooking a plunging ravine where the Ayung River snakes its way along the bottom. The losman belongs to a Balinese family that lives in a more modern house bordering the road at the front of the property. They rent out the losman for income.

When I say simple, I mean simple. The bathroom has a traditional *mandi*, a tub of cold water with a hand bucket to splash yourself with. There is no Wi-Fi and barely enough electricity to run the ceiling fans. It is often not possible to have a lamp on and the ceiling fan running at the same time. We spend our time there reading, playing board games, and cycling into the village to explore the art markets and food stalls. Renting the guesthouse includes breakfast, which has always been my favorite part of the stay. A member of the hosting family brings a tray of banana pancakes and mugs of thick, sweet, black Balinese coffee. The pancakes are out of this world. Fluffy and light with bombs of gooey warm banana and crunchy coconut shavings. I once asked Mom if Bibi could make them for us at home, but she said it wouldn't be the same eating them at home. What makes them especially magical is eating them on the round pillows in the pavilion, gazing at the view of the morning sun illuminating the rice terraces on the far side of the ravine. For a few mesmerizing minutes, the lush steppes and palms glow golden before returning to their daytime green. Often, flocks of white starlings sail down the ravine so gracefully, it seems they fly in slow motion.

Since I've been old enough, I cycle into the village by myself. I love to go and spend the afternoon in the monkey forest. It is like stepping into the pages of Rudyard Kipling's *Jungle Book* with crumbling stone walls, ropey vines, and moss-covered statues that are overrun with melodramatic monkeys. Every monkey in that forest has a yearning for the limelight. The Ubud Monkey Forest is a popular tourist spot, so the overconfident macaques have a constant audience. The crowd is kept entertained, watching the monkeys steal people's cameras or show off their tiny babies.

It was at the monkey forest that I first became interested in orangutans. A volunteer from an orangutan rescue organization was handing out brochures, hoping for donations from monkey-loving tourists. It was on the organization's Web site that I learned about the sad plight of the orangutan, the only great ape outside of Africa, right in my own backyard. It propelled me into hours of reading and research online.

So, it makes sense that it's here in Bali, sitting with my banana pancakes and gazing over the golden ravine, that the idea strikes me to start a blog. A blog about helping the orangutans, a blog about Indonesia's beautiful and fragile environment. Suddenly it all makes perfect sense. Even though I will be living away, I can continue my activism. I can continue my love for this land from afar.

Ari

A few late-afternoon patrons are finishing up their soup. Uncle and Nang are cleaning up bowls in the small kitchen. Soon they will both stop for a rest after the busy morning and lunch rush. But I know that for Uncle, there will be no rest this afternoon. Today is rescue day.

After school, I sit by Ginger Juice's cage as I have been doing for many weeks now. She still has the sarong draped over her head. I don't remember the last time I saw her eat anything. I reach through the bars and stroke her foot gently. She doesn't move away, but she also doesn't offer her hand to me as she used to do. The brutes who hurt her have taken this small pleasure away from us.

"Hold on a little longer," I whisper to her. "Today, we say good-bye. Today you will start a journey to a new life. A better life." I stop to see if she will peek at me from under her sarong, but she turns her face away from me. "I am sorry, Ginger Juice. I am sorry we did not give you a better life. You should never have been here. I understand that now." I continue to stroke her foot. "I will always think of you and pray you are living a good, healthy life. I will miss you."

A low rumble of thunder signals a warning. Billowing gray clouds fill the sky like a curtain falling. I keep an eye on the restaurant entrance for Malia. I called her as soon as I knew the rescue date. She said she was on her way home from Bali and that she would have her Oma's driver bring her. I watch the entrance and hope she arrives before the rescue crew. Heavy raindrops begin to slap noisily on the stone tiles. I move to put the hood over Elvis Presley's cage so he doesn't get wet. He is chirping a tune I do not recognize, not a human song, more like wild birdsong.

A tap on my shoulder breaks into my thoughts. And like magic, here she is, standing in front of me. The striking girl with the piercing stare. Her eyes sparkle.

"Hi, Ari," she says. "I'm Malia." She extends her hand and we shake. Her grip is firm, her hands are soft.

"Good to meet you," I say. "Thank you for coming."

"I hope I'm not late. The drive took us longer than I thought," she says with a wry smile on her lips.

"You're here in good time. The rescue team hasn't come yet." I motion toward Ginger Juice's cage. "She is still here, you see."

We walk over to her cage and Malia has an intake of breath when I point to Ginger Juice's foot protruding from the sarong. She scans the large frame under the cloth, and her eyes well with tears. "Is she sick?" she asks.

"I don't know. Ever since the attack she won't come out from under the sarong."

"An attack?" Malia face looks pale. "She was attacked? What happened?"

"Some people came in the night and poured beer over her. They also burned her with a cigarette." I look at the ground, unable to meet her eyes. "It is why I contacted you. It's why I finally realized she needs help." Moments pass as we stand next to Ginger Juice's cage. "It is bad what we have done, I know."

Malia touches my hand briefly. "But you are doing a good thing now," she says. "That is the important thing."

I look toward the restaurant and see Uncle is clearing more of the dishes and cutlery from the empty tables.

"My Uncle will not agree with you, but I think you are right." I give her a small smile. "I am grateful you are here." I usher her toward the covered area of the restaurant. "Let's get out of the rain."

And then, without warning, it begins. A parade of people file into the restaurant wearing green T-shirts with the logo of the organization called Orangutan Rescue. A uniformed police officer follows at the rear. A woman leads the group and she extends her hand to my Uncle Kus.

"Good afternoon, Sir. My name is Dr. Indrani Winarto, and I am a veterinarian. Are you the owner of this establishment?"

"Yes," he says. "What is this about?"

"We are from a local chapter of Orangutan Rescue and we have been informed an orangutan is being held here unlawfully."

Uncle reels, clearly stunned. "No," he says, "that is not true! She is mine. I won her, fair and square. Ask anyone!" He thrusts out his arms, gesturing dramatically. "Everyone around here knows that she belongs to me." He takes a challenging step toward the veterinarian. "You need to leave!"

The policeman steps from the rear of the group so that Uncle can see him.

Dr. Winarto continues in a firm but kind tone. "We understand it might come as a surprise, but keeping an orangutan in captivity is illegal."

"Illegal?" he says. "No. That cannot be. I won her from..." Uncle stops. Likely he is rethinking the notion of incriminating his army pals.

"Orangutans are wild animals, not pets," Dr. Winarto says. "It is our duty to seize the animal today. It will be taken to a rehabilitation center and given any necessary medical treatment before being sent to a sanctuary in Sumatra."

Uncle sits down heavily on one of the restaurant chairs. He looks stricken and frightened as the police officer strides toward him.

The police officer stands over Uncle Kus. He is armed

with a rifle. "We don't wish any trouble here today, Sir," he says. "I understand you did not know this was an illegal practice. If you cooperate with the rescue team, no further action will be taken." He pauses. "*If* you cooperate," he says again pointedly.

"I understand, of course," Uncle mutters, although it is clear, to avoid trouble with the authorities, he has little choice. "I will cooperate." He waves toward Ginger Juice's cage. "Take her. You have my permission."

The police officer gestures to the rescue crew to begin and he nods to Uncle. "Thank you for your cooperation, Sir. Please remain seated here while the rescue team does its work. Then we will leave you in peace."

Uncle's expression remains tense, and he sits stiffly in his seat.

Malia and I are standing a few yards away, watching the scene unfold. I am waiting for Uncle to stare at me accusingly, but he doesn't. He still has no idea it was me who made the report.

Members of the team are standing in the rain, assessing Ginger Juice's cage and what they need to do to break it open. Dr. Winarto joins them and reaches through the bars to gently remove the sarong from Ginger Juice. She is lying on her stomach, her head resting on her folded arms. The veterinarian talks to her as if she is reuniting with a long-lost friend. A volunteer holds a large umbrella over Dr. Winarto to keep the rain from pounding on her. I see Ginger Juice open her eyes briefly before burying her head in the crook of her long arms. Dr. Winarto continues to speak softly to her while she administers an injection, which I know to be a sedative. She strokes Ginger Juice's arm, still talking softly, waiting for the drug to take effect.

Uncle remains on his chair looking stunned. One of the team members goes over to him. She places brochures on the table and begins to tell him what will happen to Ginger Juice. The policeman steps back now, seeing no threat from Uncle.

"Can we listen too?" I ask.

"Of course," the woman says. "My name is Dian. I am a volunteer with Orangutan Rescue. I am telling your father..."

"My uncle," I interrupt.

"...your uncle, about what will happen to the orangutan now."

Uncle stands now, his manners apparently returned, and offers a seat to both Malia and Dian.

"Please sit down," he says. "Would you like tea? We can make you our specialty drink."

"No, thank you," says Dian. She turns back to me. "As I was saying to your uncle, the orangutan has been sedated, so we can remove her from the cage. We will then transfer her to a secure crate in the truck. Her vital signs will be monitored throughout the transfer. Dr. Winarto will examine her to determine if she requires medical treatment. Depending on her condition, she will be relocated to a care facility and rehabilitation center."

"Will she be returned to the wild?" asks Malia.

"That is the ultimate goal of our organization," the volunteer says, "but it can take years to achieve. She has not lived in the wild for a long time and will have to be reintroduced to a jungle environment. She'll have to learn how to be an orangutan again, sourcing and identifying foods, accessing water, tree climbing, nest building, and socializing with other orangutans. These are all critical skills that she'll need to relearn in order to survive in the wild. Hopefully, one day she will live free once again."

"I didn't know there were organizations that did this kind of work. It is a good thing," Uncle says to the volunteer. "We tried our best, you know. When she was little, we treated her like a real baby. It was later, when she got bigger—she was so strong. I was scared she would get hurt." He shakes his head. "Perhaps I should have sent her to you a long time ago."

I can hardly believe my ears. I am not sure if Uncle is saying this to save face in front of the volunteer, or if he truly means it. Perhaps Uncle Kus isn't sure either.

"May I ask you a question?" he asks Dian, and she nods. "Who called you to say there was an orangutan here? Was it one of the patrons? All of my guests love her so much."

My heart pounds. Surely Uncle can see the guilt written on my face.

"We cannot give that information," Dian replies. "I'm sorry."

The noise of a chainsaw interrupts our conversation.

We all go to stand a safe distance from the cage while the team cuts through the bars. Malia takes photos with her phone. The vet holds a stethoscope to Ginger Juice's chest. She is limp, clearly asleep from the drug. I am grateful she is spared the loud noise and trauma of being moved. It takes many team members to place her on the stretcher once the cage is broken. I watch in awe. Her size and mass appear altered outside of the cage. She looks so much bigger. I look to Uncle, who is visibly shaken.

"It will be OK," I tell him. "She will be taken to a better place. She deserves a better life than this. It was time."

Sudden recognition of my betrayal crosses his face. Now he understands it was me. Now he fully grasps what I have done, and I brace myself for his fury.

Malia

No one objects as I take out my phone to document Ginger Juice's liberation. Rain continues to lash down. I take photos as best I can as she is lifted from the cage. She remains sedated as she is placed on a large stretcher. I am in awe being so close to an orangutan. Even asleep, she is truly an amazing creature. Seeing the rescue unfold reaffirms my desire to help save more like her.

I go back to the covered area to speak with Ari, but he is standing with his uncle. Ari looks utterly despairing, and I wish I could do or say something to smooth the edges of his worry.

I notice Dian standing to the side and take the opportunity to speak with her out of their earshot.

"May I have a copy of your brochures?" I ask her. "I am very interested in activism for orangutans."

"Of course," she says, handing me the pamphlets. "That is good to know. We can use all the help we can get. Are you a family friend?"

"No. I met Ari through a petition I circulated against anti-palm labels."

"So, you really are one of us." She grins.

Ginger Juice is being carefully loaded into the rescue truck. Ari has now gone to stand next the vehicle, watching over her intently. I gesture to the scene unfolding. "How do you think this happens?" I ask quietly. "I mean, hundreds of people must have been to this warung and seen Ginger Juice in the cage. How could no one do anything to help her?"

Dian shakes her head sadly. "It often happens in these small towns. An animal is kept out in the open like this, so people assume that there is nothing wrong with it and the animal is properly cared for. They don't realize the consequences of keeping a wild animal in a cage." She leans closer to me. "I also believe this warung is frequented by many of the local military, so I'm sure no one would have wanted to cause any trouble. This is also common. We see a lot of orangutans kept by military personnel. It can be viewed as a kind of status symbol." She pauses. "But all it takes is for one person to decide to do something—for one person to make a telephone call."

"So, I guess it is really true," I say. "One person can make a difference."

"Yes," she says. "But having more people is better."

On the ride home, the Mercedes gets stuck in the flooding. The heavy rain has made the main road from Malang to Surabaya inaccessible. Gamin does a mighty job guiding the Mercedes through back alleys and dirt roads. Water from the rain is unsettlingly high.

"How do you know these back roads so well?" I ask him.

"I grew up near Malang," he says. "I know these roads. But they are not good for this car." He shakes his head. "It would have been much better if we came on my motorbike."

I smile to myself. He is right, but there is no way Oma would have allowed me to ride on the back of a motorcycle. Thankfully, the Mercedes stays above the water, but it is slow going. I wind down the car window and watch village children playing in the street that has turned into a small river. The rainwater is up to their skinny knees. I watch them laughing, splashing each other with the brown water, and I think about the day. It was exhilarating, but also emotionally difficult and confusing.

When I first arrived at the warung and saw such a magnificent creature in that small cage, it broke my heart. But seeing Ari's kind face with such a tortured expression stopped me from saying the obvious things, like "This is terrible. How could you do this? How could you let this creature suffer?" Even when he told me about the awful attack that occurred,

I could see he was steeped in guilt, and words of accusation would be cruel. I tried to use words of comfort instead, hoping they would help.

Ari's uncle appeared to be a nice enough man. It is hard to imagine he would keep an orangutan as a pet. I listened to him explain the situation of how he came to put Ginger Juice in the cage, and I'm still not sure what to think. Was it laziness? Ignorance? Did he simply not realize she could have a better life, that she could be sent to a sanctuary and maybe one day returned to the wild? From the confusion on Ari's face, I could see that he was not sure of his uncle's motivations either.

Before I left, I thanked Ari for letting me be there.

"It's because of your petition that this happened at all," he said. "It is I who should thank you."

I hope Ari knows how brave I think he is. I tried to tell him, but it was such a hectic day.

I wave good-bye to village kids as the car finally climbs to dry road. We are speeding toward Surabaya again, and I feel good knowing that my petition had a positive impact after all. My role in Ginger Juice's rescue was very small, but I am proud of my part. And I already have my first blog post written in my mind. I know exactly who it will be dedicated to.

Ari

It's over. Malia has left, and the rescue team has driven away with Ginger Juice. Uncle and I are left standing, looking at the empty, broken cage.

"Elvis Presley will be taken as well," I say to Uncle. "I found a bird sanctuary in Batubulan. They will collect him this week."

Uncle Kus does not speak. I have been waiting for him to explode with anger. His silence is unnerving. I fill the void with my own chatter, hoping to spill all that I want to say before he erupts.

"I am sorry, Uncle. I hope you do not take my actions as disrespect, but I could not bear to see Ginger Juice in distress any longer. It had been building and building within me, ever since I came here, seeing her in this cage. It did not feel right. Her eyes, when they followed me, they drilled into me. And then...and then," I stammer. "After the incident when she was burned, I knew she had to be rescued."

"How could I know?" he asks. He rubs his eyes, but they remain dry. "How could I know there were people who could take better care of her? I thought we were giving her the best we could. Why didn't you speak with me first? How could you do this without coming to me first?"

I study my Uncle's face. He looks humiliated. He is upset, but he is not angry.

"Because I knew you would say no," I say.

Uncle Kus turns his head for a moment. He knows this is to be true.

"I found some information on a petition," I go on. "I found it when I went to the chess tournament in Surabaya. It was from the girl who was here. Malia."

"The bule girl?"

"She's not a foreigner, she has lived here her whole life. Her mother is Canadian, her father Indonesian. She is very committed to saving orangutans."

Uncle looks at the mangled enclosure.

"I will help you take away this cage. When the patrons arrive in the morning, it won't be here. You can tell them Ginger Juice has gone back to the jungle where she belongs."

His expression lightens at the prospect of saving face with his patrons. "Yes. Yes. I can tell them I have given her to

the sanctuary people for her good health. For her own good."
He pauses. "I only ever wanted what was best for her."

I am genuinely unsure if he believes what he is saying, but
it is certain that he needs *me* to believe it, and he needs his
patrons to believe it too.

"Of course," I say. "I know you cared about her."

"Yes," he nods. "Yes, I did. We all did." He is holding the
brochure that Dian gave him. "Did you know that many orangutans have been released back to the jungle? I will tell my friends
about this." He shakes the papers. "They should all know about
this work. They should all have this information."

I nod my agreement.

"I didn't understand," he says, shaking his head. "I didn't
know."

We both continue to look at the empty cage. I know that
what is closer to truth is that he didn't *want* to understand.
He didn't *want* to know.

I have learned that it is possible to ignore truths that are
right under your nose. You can choose to ignore them, or you
can speak up.

And now, I have more truths that need to be brought to
light. My time of being silent is over.

Malia

A week after the rescue, I dial the telephone number for Warung Malang. A woman, likely the kitchen helper, answers the telephone after many rings and says she will call Ari to the phone. A breathless Ari comes on the line after a few minutes.

"Hello, Malia! How are you?" It is good to hear Ari's voice sound so much lighter than before.

"I'm good, thanks. How are you? I was just wondering if you've heard any news about Ginger Juice?"

"I'm glad you called, Malia," he says. "On the rescue day it was such a rush. I'm sorry I didn't thank you properly for coming to support me. You've helped me more than you realize. I'm really grateful."

"You did thank me," I say. "But I know what you mean. A lot was going on that day." I pause for a moment. "I wanted to tell you as well how brave I thought you were for doing what was right. I know it's wasn't easy."

There is a pause on the other end, but I know Ari is pleased to hear what I have said.

"Thank you," I hear him say quietly.

"So, do you have news about Ginger Juice?" I ask.

"Yes, I do." Ari clears his throat. "Dr. Winarto called to tell us that Ginger Juice is being looked after at the care facility in Yogakarta. After an examination, they found that she was in fair health, thank goodness, aside from being overweight. She's being put on a special diet. Her mental health is another thing. She has anxious behaviors, which they say are typical of apes that have been held in captivity. The vet said it can take a long time for the emotional and mental well-being of an orangutan to heal.

"Once she is strong enough, they'll transfer her to a sanctuary in Sumatra. Dr. Winarto said she is a Sumatran orangutan. In the sanctuary, with luck, she'll learn how to be an orangutan again. I will keep you updated when I know more."

"Wow. That's great to hear. Such fantastic news. Please do keep me updated. I know you have my e-mail." We both chuckle, remembering. "I'm moving to Canada soon, but I hope we can stay in touch."

I tell him about my plans to write a blog. I don't tell him about the dedication, I want it to be a surprise.

"Canada! That is big news. I'd definitely like to stay in touch and read your blog. I might have news of my own to share with you soon as well," he says, mysteriously.

"Well don't keep me hanging for too long," I tell him.

Ari

I sit nervously in the school administrator's office. I have never been here before. I don't know if my plan will work, but I have to try.

"Come in, Ari," the school administrator says as he takes the seat behind his desk. "How can I help you today?"

"Thank you, Sir," I say. "I have a matter...um, that I hope...I can...." I am stuck.

The school administrator watches me patiently. "Why don't you just tell me what you need, and I'll see what I can do?"

I nod and swallow. "Thank you, Sir. I am very nervous."

"I can see that, Ari. What is making you nervous?"

I think for a moment. I think about why I am here. I think about the guilty feelings that have been gnawing away at me since I started school.

"I did something I wish I had not done and now, I want to make it right," I say finally.

"This sounds like it will be quite a story," he says, leaning back in his chair. "Why don't you start at the beginning."

I tell him about Suni and how we grew up together in the village. About our parents, who are rice farmers, but how they don't own the land they farm. They are tenant farmers so they don't earn much money from the crops. The wealth from the crops benefits the landowners and large food companies instead. Then I tell him how special Suni is, how curious and clever she is. How excited she becomes at the prospect of learning new things. How she used to stay up past midnight working on her school assignments by candlelight. How she would still be first up, dressed, and ready for elementary school, her uniform pressed and her satchel neatly packed. And then I tell him how, when our parents presented me with my middle-school enrollment form, she had hugged me with genuine love, so happy for me. And how I later saw her bent over, silently sobbing in her room. She had let herself hope, but the hope was gone. I had taken it.

"It should be Suni here at school," I tell him. "Not me."

"Why don't you think you deserve to be here?" he asks.

"It's not that I don't deserve it," I say. "I wish we could both be here. But our situation doesn't afford it. We always knew only one of us would have the money for further schooling. My parents and hers thought it more important for me to go to school, because I am a boy." I pause. "But I think that is wrong. I think Suni should be here. She should be given the opportunity instead of me. I want her to take my place."

"I appreciate your sentiments toward your cousin, Ari. But it is important for you to continue your studies. You are a good student, I can't support you dropping out of school." He shuffles some papers around on his desk. "And what about your parents? You would need to have their permission."

"If you can make the switch possible," I say. "I will explain it to them. They will understand. My schooling will just be delayed, and I will enroll again, once I have earned the money to attend." I sit forward in my chair. "Can I tell you something else, Sir?"

"Of course."

"I have learned something very important while I have been here," I say. "Well, I have learned many things in my studies, of course, but what I am talking about hasn't to do with my classes."

"Oh, really? What is it you have learned?" he asks.

"Chess," I say and he raises his eyebrows for me to go on.

"I learned how to play chess," I say. "It is a marvelous game, Sir, do you know it?"

He shakes his head. "Just a little."

"Chess taught me the value of patience. It taught me that there are many ways to reach your goal. There's millions of strategies and moves you can plan ahead in order to achieve what you want." I take a breath. "I can be patient, Sir. I can play a long game and find my way back to school."

I pull three chess pieces from my satchel.

"If I were to look at this problem as a chess game," I go on. "Suni would be a pawn." I place the pawn piece on the desk in front of the administrator. "A pawn does not have much power and she can only take single steps. If another piece blocks her path, she is stuck, she cannot move." I then place a knight on the table, in front of the pawn.

"In this scenario, I could be represented by a knight. A knight is able to move more freely around the board. He can jump over other pieces and he can go forward and backwards. The knight's job is to clear the path."

I move the pawn in front of the knight. "Because you see, the pawn, even though she has little power, has great potential. If her path is cleared and she makes her way to the other side of the board, she can become promoted."

The administrator looks at me quizzically.

"Being promoted means she becomes a queen," I say. "And the queen is the most powerful piece of all." I stand the last chess piece, the queen, on my open palm. "So, you see, I am a knight, and I am simply clearing a path for a future queen."

We both are silent for a few moments, looking at the queen piece I am offering to him.

The school administrator rubs his chin, and a small smile escapes his lips. "You have a unique way of looking at your situation, Ari. And you have given me a lot to think about.

Let me take this under advisement. I will see what I can do, but I cannot make any promises. This is very unorthodox." He reaches across his desk to shake my hand. "You are a fine young man, Ari," he says.

"I hope to be, Sir," I say, returning his handshake. "That is also part of the plan."

Malia

Bibi spends part of each weekend with her family, back in her village. She leaves after breakfast on Saturday and returns late Sunday evening.

"Will you teach me how to make my own bubur?" I ask Bibi when she comes in to wake me up on Saturday morning. "And can I come with you when you visit your family in the village today? I want to know where I can think of you being when we're gone."

Bibi swats at some stray tears she doesn't want me to see and grips my arm tightly. She takes me back to the kitchen. I'm still in my pajamas.

The kitchen is not a room I have spent much time in. It is Bibi's domain. The smell of chicken porridge fills the small room. I notice her radio is playing a local station. Steam rises as she lifts the lid from a pot on the stove. I peer in and see white rice boiling down to the mushy consistency of porridge.

"Here. You slice the shallots," she says, hovering at my shoulder. "No. Thinner," she demands, making *tsk-tsk* noises at my bad slicing skills. She heats some oil in a fry pan and gestures for me to add the shallots to it. "It's hot! Careful you don't burn them!" It takes only seconds for them to brown, and Bibi whips the saucepan off the stove top. Next comes sliced green onion and shredded chicken that she magically produces from plastic containers. "Stir it all in," she says. "Quick, while it's hot." She makes large stir motions in case, for some reason, I don't understand.

"But I need to know how to do it from the beginning," I tell her. "This is already done. I'm just stirring the ingredients together."

She shakes her head impatiently. "You won't need to know how to make bubur when you're in Canada. You'll eat Canadian breakfast there."

I think on this for a while. *Will I? I hope I will keep eating my favorite Indonesian foods when I'm in Canada.*

"Bubur will be waiting for you when you come back," she says.

Usually Bibi takes a patchwork of buses, minivans, and pedicabs to get to her village, but today Mom drives us there. It takes an hour driving on winding, bumpy, potholed roads. "How long does it usually take you?" I ask Bibi.

She holds up three fingers. "Three hours if no rain," she says matter-of-factly.

I shake my head at all the things about Bibi that I have never thought about. When she was away from our house, she ceased to exist for me. I have never once thought about how long it took her to get to the village, or what she did when she got there.

Bibi sees my look of consternation. She flaps her hand at me and says, "This is normal."

After climbing up a steep hill with rice fields on both sides of the road, we pull up in front of a small house that backs onto a dense patch of forest. Banana trees are planted next to the gate, and a few chickens scratch around in the dirt yard. "This is it," Mom says.

"You've been here before?" I ask her.

"Of course," she says. "Papa bought this house for Bibi years ago. You've been here too. You were just too little to remember it."

Soon a stream of smiling faces pours out of the small house. All of them are deliriously happy to see Bibi. They hug her and lift the bags from her shoulders and shoo her inside the house. Bibi is treated like royalty here. She is the queen returning to her castle.

We are led into the living room and given warm, sweet tea in glasses. Dishes of salty peanuts and slices of moist cake are laid out on small tables. People from nearby houses drop by to pay their respects to Bibi and, no doubt, are curious to meet Mom and me too. All are introduced as relatives. A gaggle of tiny children wobbles around us with fists full of cake. Bibi's grandchildren, we are told. Bibi sits proudly on a leather armchair that I recognize as an old chair of Papa's. She is beaming with pride over the scene. To see Bibi smiling is unusual for me. I realize I have not seen her so relaxed before. She is the matriarch of her family and seeing this delights me. This is how I will always picture her.

"We are so glad that our mother will be home with us soon," says a pretty woman, introduced to us as Bibi's daughter-in-law. "We have been wanting her to stop working for years, but she was adamant that she was still needed in the city."

"I can't imagine my life without her," I admit. "She helped raise me."

I look over at Bibi who is now cradling a small infant in her arms. She is clucking at the baby and rocking it back and forth. "Bibi is home now. Bibi will take care of you," she coos to it.

I smile to myself. And to think, once upon a time, I'd thought she'd be lost without me.

Ari

I ring the ox bell to let my family know I am home. I see my mother and father look up from their work in the rice fields. They cover their eyes from the sun to see who has rung the bell. I wave enthusiastically with both of my arms overhead and they drop their work, gesturing excitedly that they are coming to meet me. Before they reach the house, I feel a tap on my shoulder. I turn around and see it is Suni. My cousin, my friend, the prankster I have missed so much.

"It's you! You're home," she says. "Took you long enough." We embrace. "How long can you stay?" she asks.

"I am home for good," I tell her.

"Wah! What do you mean?" She slaps my shoulder playfully. "You have school. What about helping at Uncle's warung?"

"I have arranged for someone else to take my place," I say.

"Who could do that?" she asks, her eyes squinting with suspicion. "What are you talking about?"

I make sure she is looking at my face, so she knows I am not lying. She can always tell if I am lying. "You, of course," I say. "You. It is your turn to go to school. It should have been you all along."

I leave a stunned Suni—her mouth open like a koi fish—to embrace my parents who have made their way in from the fields.

"Ari, my son! Such a wonderful surprise." My mother throws her arms around my neck. "And it isn't even Friday! I haven't cooked your favorite *longton sayur lodeh*." We all laugh.

"Our son has returned. Come. Sit, sit," my father says, wiping his brow. The hard work of the fields is visible on his face. "Come and tell us all of your news."

"I have a lot to tell you," I say, allowing my parents to fuss over me. "There is a lot to explain."

Suni makes tea, keeping her ear to the conversation as she pours boiling water over dry tea leaves in the big metal teapot. My parents and I sit on the well-worn chairs on the covered verandah. Suni's parents, my aunt and uncle, soon join us.

"Nephew!" they exclaim, treating me like celebrity. "Look at you! So grown up now. You look like a man, no longer a boy."

I gaze at the smiling faces of my family beaming at me, and I feel so happy to be home. We blow steam from the fresh tea

that Suni has poured, and I tell them my news. I am relieved
to confess what I have done. The plans I have put into action.
I'm sure they will argue, but I have my counter strategies ready.

The school administrator agreed that Suni will take my
place at middle school for the remainder of the year, but he
was adamant that next year he expects us both to be enrolled.
It is a condition that I wholly agreed to. The fact is, it is Suni
who needs to do her schooling now, not me. As a boy, I have
more options, more freedoms. If Suni goes to school now, she
can later choose if she wants to continue her studies or find a
career or return here if she wishes. She will not be forced to stay
without opportunities available to her, or get married early like
her friends are already talking about doing. At least she will
have choices.

I will find paid work to raise money for my own school fees,
something Suni's parents would not feel comfortable with her
doing. I will help my parents in the fields and continue to study
chess and set my sights on qualifying for an international tournament one day.

No longer consumed with worry for Ginger Juice, I have
returned to my interest in chess. My early beginner's luck gave
me a glimpse into what might be possible if I dedicate myself
to the game. Our school did not win the tournament. I wish
I could have been there to support the team, but there will be
more games, more tournaments.

I have no regrets. I still have many strategies to learn and
many plans to put into place. Most importantly, I have patience
for the long game.

Ginger Juice

Open eyes and think I dream. Dream from before-life when back in forest, back in sway of treetops with humming, whirring, buzzing jungle.

Reach hand out but do not feel bars of cage.

Where they go?

Reach out with feet and still do not feel bars. Blink eyes. Do not trust the green all around. Do not believe soft rustle of branches above.

Close eyes again. This is trick. Cannot be right. Haze wants trick me.

Michelle Kadarusman

Lie still. Very still. Can still hear *woosh, woosh*. Must find out! Try again.

I reach out, slowly, slowly with arms and feet to find bars. Still no bars. But touch something else. Fingers remember this touch. Is dirt. Why dirt is in my cage?

And what scent this is? This scent like earth, moss, and leaves. I take big, big breath of this scent. Breathe deep, deep into belly and it lights color in my mind. *Hhk, hhk!*

Open eyes again and this time see where I am. Canopy of leaves sways high above me. Blink, blink at sunspots dancing between palms and see butterflies kissing tiny orchid petals. Hear far off *wa-wa* echo from gibbon and *trill* and *whip* of songbirds. And now, yes, *buzz, buzzing* of cicadas, katydids, and crickets.

I back in the forest again!

Slow Loris Boy understood me. I tried tell the humans many, many times. But Slow Loris did it.

He take me home.

Ari

I've had news from the orangutan rescue organization with an update on Ginger Juice. She has been moved to a rehabilitation center in Sumatra. It's a kind of jungle school, like Dian told us about, where orphaned and captive orangutans learn how to survive in the wild again.

Ginger Juice has been regaining her physical strength and is also showing more confidence. She has even started to make her own tree nests and forage for her own food. It might take years, but they believe she is a very good candidate for being released back into the wild one day.

The welcome news from Orangutan Rescue about Ginger

Juice's good progress at jungle school is made better by having Malia to share it with. She e-mailed me back saying she can't keep the smile from her face after reading it. And now, neither can I.

I spend my mornings in the rice fields, helping my parents, aunt, and uncle with the never-ending chores of farming. I am responsible for feeding the ducks and the water buffalo. When I see saplings clumped together, I separate them, spacing them out and replanting them to even out the crop. It is tiring work, but there is also comfort working alongside my family with the cool squelch of mud under my feet and a sea of shimmering jade-green shoots before me.

In the afternoons, I have a job in the village, helping at the photocopy shop. The shop is next door to the Internet Café, so I am able to keep in contact with Malia, Faisel, and my chess buddies by e-mail.

I have also found many Web sites to help me with my self-directed chess studies. With no willing opponents in the village, I have been playing chess online. My goal to one day qualify for an international tournament shines brightly ahead, beckoning me like a golden sunrise.

Suni bubbles with news each time I open my e-mail. She has taken to schoolwork like a duck to water, as I knew she would. She has also become friends with Melonie and Samir, as I had imagined. No doubt the girls have taken my cousin under their wing. They all urge me to be diligent about saving my earnings so I can rejoin them next year.

Uncle is pleased with this arrangement as well. Suni has updated his printed menus and the customers are charmed with her presence at the warung. Suni says, save for some small children, no one asks about Ginger Juice. Uncle's customers are not disappointed at his missing "attractions." I'm sure his customers are also relieved that Ginger Juice and Elvis Presley are free of their cages.

I was honored that Malia dedicated her first blog post to me. I continue to read all of her posts with great interest. In her latest one she wrote about saving the forest habitat for orangutans. She wrote about farmers producing crops under the rainforest canopy, instead of clearing the land for crops such as rice or palm oil. There are other crops—spices, vanilla, and honey—that can thrive under the tree canopy without destroying the rainforest. Plus, profits from the crops don't have to be shared with large corporations, as farmers can sell their goods directly to markets.

I read this information with great interest and plan to discuss it with my father, my uncle, and our neighbors. Most evenings, the men sit around to debate and decide how best to manage the land we own or manage. As Malia tells it, agriculture under the rainforest canopy is good for everyone, the farmers and the orangutans. I am excited to share these possibilities with my village community.

My world feels light again. I no longer have to push away unwanted feelings of guilt. My heart is full, my conscience is free. I am excited about the future, and the futures of those I love.

Some nights I walk out into the rice paddies to lie under the stars, as Suni once wrote she used to do. I feel the warm earth beneath me and breathe in the heady fragrance from the coconut and frangipani trees. I listen to the orchestra of frogs croaking in the rice gullies and imagine my hand is resting in Ginger Juice's huge palm. I see her soft eyes as I watch the flickering pinpoints of light above me.

The universe is a large and wondrous place, and I know that for now, just like Ginger Juice and Suni, I am exactly where I should be.

Malia

Oma, Mom, and I go together to sit under the mango tree.

Mom and I will fly to Toronto tomorrow, and we have finally finished all of our packing. The household furniture is being sent in a big shipping container. We will just take our suitcases full of clothing on the airplane. Mom says I'll have to buy a lot of new clothes anyway, to suit the cooler weather in Canada. I like this idea. A new wardrobe, a new Malia. Maybe a bright red raincoat and matching leather boots? It's a version of myself I have not imagined before and it gives me a shimmer of excitement.

We brush off the fallen leaves from Papa's grave, and I place a bunch of tuberoses on the stone. Perhaps it is because I am not alone, but I don't hear Papa's voice in my head as I usually do when I come here. We all sit with our own thoughts for a while, and I take Mom's hand. She squeezes it. I know this is a difficult day for her. To my surprise Oma takes Mom's other hand, and I see a look pass between them. It's a look of gratitude and understanding. A look of a shared love, maybe not for each other, but for Papa. And for me.

As we get up to leave, I trace Papa's name that is etched into the headstone. I look at the fresh flowers, glad that Oma will be here to continue caring for our shrine.

"I think Papa has gone ahead to Canada," I say to Mom. "I think maybe he is already swimming in the lake and pointing out a pair of loons drifting by."

"He was an excellent swimmer," Oma says proudly.

Mom kisses the top of my head. "I think you're right," she says. "He always liked to be the first one in the lake." We smile at each other. "Such a show off, your Papa," she says.

I know I will find him there. Just as I will find him wherever I am.

Ginger Juice

This place, it is not *our* jungle. But it is still jungle. Other apes here too. We watch each other, we signal each other. *We are here to get well,* one old ape tells me. *We are here to get strong again. Some of us are too old and weak to leave, but you are still young.*

Humans here too, but they do not put me in cage. They sit and watch me but do not poke me or hurt me. These humans put fruit on high places in treetops so I have to climb to get it. Slow, slow I feel arms and legs get strong. Slow, slow, I can climb higher every day. Maybe this why humans leave the food in higher and higher places for me to climb.

I like to sit and feel sun on my shoulders. Long, long time not feel this warm feeling. This good feeling. Spend long, long time just sitting to feel the sun again.

Climb to high, high platform and think will not go back down to forest floor. I make nest in treetops, just like you teach me long ago in before-life.

I choose branches, thick with leaves, and thin saplings. Weave together soft bed. Sit in nest now and look over forest canopy. I see gentle mist hover below tips of giant fig trees. Watch treeswifts hop from branch to branch and see forest ants march up and down silver trunks. I breathe in scent of damp earth and cinnamon bark.

Haze does not come for me here.

Maybe soon go look for rambutan and papaya like we used to do. Maybe soon leave this place and find our own jungle like we used to have. More time I spend in treetop nest, more far away human world is.

I go less and less for food humans put on platforms. Spend time high above ground, but sometimes like to see what fruit humans leave. Sometimes like watch for other apes or look at humans from safety of high branch.

Look now, and see old ape sitting in ray of sunshine on forest floor, where humans leave bananas and jackfruit. Her face turns to sun. Her eyes do not see, she has many scars. But my eyes see. They know her shape. I look long, long time.

Climb down slow from high branch to forest floor and move closer, closer.

BERANI

Heart hammers fast, fast, like woodpecker's beak against tree trunk, because I know her breath. I know her scent.

Move so close. Gently place head on her chest.

You open your arms, Ibu, and I still fit there, even though not little ape anymore. I still fit in place under your arm. We still fit together, just like always did.

You and me, Ibu. We together again.

Your hand strokes my head and you whisper my name. Name I can never make humans understand. Name you give to me.

Berani.

Berani means brave.

Glossary

Asli – Original

Becak – An Indonesian three-wheeled pedicab. It has a seat at the front and the driver pedals the bicycle wheels at the rear. It is a common and inexpensive way to get around many Indonesian cities and towns.

Berani – Brave

Buntut – Tail

Bubur – An Indonesian congee, or rice porridge, usually made with white rice chicken and flavored with spices. It is a common breakfast food.

Bule – a slang Indonesian word for foreigners, especially people from western countries or white/Caucasians.

Campuran – Mixed

Dangdut – A genre of music that is a mix of Indonesian folk, traditional, and popular music.

Ibu – Mother or Mrs.

Jeruk – A citrus fruit that is commonly referred to as an orange.

Mie goreng – *mie:* noodles *goreng:* fried. Fried noodles is a very popular Indonesian dish. The noodles are often flavored with vegetables, chicken, meat, or seafood.

Nasi goreng – *nasi:* rice, *goreng:* fried. Fried rice is a very popular Indonesian dish. The rice is often flavored with vegetables, chicken, meat, or seafood. Often a fried egg is served on top.

Orang asli – Spoken to describe a native Indonesian, or indigenous, person.

Orang – Person

Orangutan – Forest person; or person of the forest.

Sarong – A traditional cloth worn by women and men throughout Southeast Asia. A sarong is made from batik cloth or printed cotton and shaped in a large rectangle. A sarong can be wrapped to create a variety of styles of dress. It has multiple other uses, from blanket to baby sling.

Selamat sore – Good afternoon

Sekolah Menegah Pertama – first high school, or what western countries refer to as middle school.

Sop – *Soup*

Utan – Forest

Warung – A small restaurant or food stall.

Orangutans

Orangutans are found on the islands of Sumatra and Borneo. They are the only Great Apes found outside of Africa and the largest tree-dwelling beings in the world.

There are three distinct species: the Sumatran orangutan (*Pongo abelii*), the Borneo orangutan (*Pongo pigmaeus*), and the Tapanuli orangutan (*Pongo tapanuliensis*).

Fully grown males can weigh between 200 to 300 pounds and females 100 to 120 pounds. They have been recorded to live up to 60 years of age.

Orangutans share up to 97% of human DNA and are known to be exceptionally intelligent.

Orangutans are primarily fruit eaters and, in the wild, spend most of their time in the tree canopy foraging upon a wide variety of wild vegetation.

Orangutans are critically endangered. It is estimated that fewer than 100,000 are currently living in the wild, and up to 3,000 are killed each year. In the next ten years, if orangutans don't have enough rainforest habitat, they could be lost forever.

ORANGUTAN RESCUE

The orangutan population is so small that each individual orangutan is valuable. Each orangutan that is being held in captivity should be liberated and rehabilitated so it may have a chance to return to the wild population and continue the species' survival.

ORANGUTAN HABITAT

Lowland areas that are good for farming are also the best habitat for orangutans. Nutrients flow downhill to the fruit trees in the lowland areas. This means that agriculture and orangutans will always be in competition. It is a competition that orangutans have been losing, and losing very badly, for many years.

It is simple to blame palm-oil farmers who destroy the orangutan habitat, but the farmers alone are not to blame. They are simply trying to make a living. It is the massive agricultural corporations who make the decisions of what to plant in order to return the most profit. Once a rainforest has been cleared for *monoculture* farming, the orangutan habitat has been destroyed.

WHAT IS MONOCULTURE?

Monoculture is any single crop, like palm oil or rice or rubber or coconut palms. When you hear about *sustainable palm oil*, it is better than unsustainable palm oil because it means it is farmed responsibly, but it has already destroyed orangutan habitat.

SOLUTIONS

Solutions are needed that will preserve the remaining rainforests and provide farmers with alternative incomes. Rainforests need to be secured to protect these unique ecosystems and their endangered species—not just orangutans, but elephants and tigers as well.

It takes activism to raise awareness and to raise donations to make it happen. Education is also needed to empower land owners with other options like under-tree-canopy farming. Crops such as vanilla, honey, and spices can be farmed without destroying the rainforest.

HOW CAN WE HELP?

As a consumer, not buying products that include palm oil is a good thing, but it will not, on its own, save the orangutans.

We all have an individual responsibility to make meaningful choices every day to help the planet; what we buy does have an impact, but we can make other everyday decisions:

- We can recycle and avoid using single-use plastic products. Use reusable water bottles.
- We can have a minimal carbon footprint by walking or riding a bike instead of driving, when possible.
- We can use renewable energy, such as wind and solar power.
- We can be aware of water conservation by making sure to turn off the tap while brushing our teeth.

- We can turn lights off when we leave a room.
- And we can choose to use our voice to raise awareness for change.

Every day we can be conscious of our actions and how they impact the planet.

The Orangutan Project (TOP) works tirelessly on initiatives to help save the species. TOP is a highly effective organization making dramatic investments in saving orangutans and rain forests.

Their work focuses on these areas:
1. Rescue, Rehabilitation, Release
2. Securing and Protecting Natural Habitat
3. Educating and Supporting Local Communities
4. Changing the Game by Standing Up and Speaking Out

If you would like to make a donation or read more about the good work they do, here is the website:

www.orangutan.org.au

Author's note

This story was inspired by an experience I had when I was living in Surabaya, Indonesia many years ago.

My brother was also living in Indonesia at the time and traveling to remote areas of East Java for his work. He called me one day, distressed, to tell me he had been to a small restaurant in the village of Malang, East Java, where he saw an orangutan in a cage.

These were the days before Google. It wasn't a simple thing to find an orangutan rescue organization, plus, the small restaurant itself didn't have a regular street address, so we knew it would be hard to find again.

I spoke with my friends in Surabaya and asked if anyone could help us rescue the orangutan. Luckily, a friend knew of someone who volunteered for an animal rescue organization. My friend promised to get in touch for me.

Weeks went by and one day the volunteer called me. The rescue organization would be in the Malang area that very day and needed to know immediately where the orangutan was being held. I was in a panic to find my brother. (These were the days before cell phones!) When I managed to track him down, he had to explain the location in detail so they could find it.

We both waited, very anxious, hoping that the volunteer would be able to find the orangutan.

She was found and rescued from the cage that she had been held in for many years. Just like in the story, the cage had to be cut open to release her as she had outgrown the opening.

My brother returned to the restaurant weeks later. He spoke with the owner about the orangutan. The owner was relieved that she had been rescued. He had not known how to care for her and had not known that organizations worked to rescue, rehabilitate, and release orangutans.

We were grateful that he had cooperated with the organization, and that the orangutan was rescued.

I don't know what happened to that orangutan once she was rescued. My dearest hope is that she is still alive today, living wild and free in a rainforest in Sumatra or Borneo. As all orangutans should be.

Acknowledgments

I have learned so much about orangutans and have many to thank for their guidance, knowledge, and wisdom on the topic. Thanks to Anitha Rao Robinson, a Director of the Wildlife Conservation International Foundation Canada, and to Leif Cocks, the founder of The Orangutan Project. Leif's book, *Orangutans, My cousins, My friends* (The Orangutan Project, 2016), was especially helpful, along with his informative webinars. Thanks to the Orangutan Sanctuary at the Melbourne Zoo, Australia. While COVID-19 prevented me from traveling to Indonesia as I had planned to do, I am grateful to have spent time at the Melbourne Zoo Orangutan Sanctuary to observe the three stunning orangutans there: Kiani, Gabby, and Malu. Thanks to my primatology fact reader, Felicia Epstein. Any errors are my own.

I am grateful for the financial support I received from the Canada Council for the Arts and the Ontario Arts Council to research and write this story.

Thanks to my first reader, Sophia Christou.

So very grateful to my editor, Kathryn Cole. And to Associate Editor Erin Alladin.

Special thanks to my dream publisher, Gail Winskill, and to the Pajama Press team.

Forever and always thanks to my family, Teddy, Sophia, and Mark.